ALSO BY KIME

Notebook Myster

Notebook Mysteries ~ Decisions and Possibilities (Book 2)

Notebook Mysteries ~ Changes and Challenges (Book 3)

Notebook Mysteries ~ Unexpected Outcomes (Book 4)

Notebook Mysteries ~ Haunted Christmas (a novella)

Notebook Mysteries ~ Suspicions (Book 5)

Notebook Mysteries ~ Parisian Intrigue (Book 6)

Notebook Mysteries ~ A Party to Remember (a Novella)

Notebook Mysteries ~ Art of Deception (Book 7)

Notebook Mysteries ~ The Twelve days of Murder (a Novella)

Stand alone books:

Divided Lives (pen name K.R. Mullins)

Lights, Camera, Murder!!!

1897 A Mark Sutherland Adventure

Notebook Mysteries

Notebook Mysteries

The Twelve Days
of
Murder

KIMBERLY
MULLINS

NOTEBOOK MYSTERIES ~ THE TWELVE DAYS OF MURDER

Notebook Mysteries Series

First edition: December 2024

Mailing address for JKJ books, LLC; 17350 State Highway 249, STE 220 #3515 Houston, Texas 77064

Library of Congress Control Number: 2024921903

ISBN (paperback): 979-8-9916865-4-9

ISBN (hardback): 979-8-9916865-5-6

ISBN (ebook): 979-8-9916865-3-2

This is a work of fiction. It is based on historical events within Chicago during the time period of the 1880-90's.

Edited by Kaitlyn Katsoupis, Strictly Textual

Cover Art by Miblart

Christmas is a wonderful time for family, friends and excellent movies. And by the way Die Hard IS a Christmas movie. Much love to Jonathan, Joshua and my close friend Claudia.

NOTES FROM AUTHOR

There are 23 versions of the song The Twelve Days of Christmas. The first was published in 1790 and the last in 1966. The one I am using is the 1891 version. This one is the closest to my date, the book is set in 1891.

Kidson, 1891

On the first day of Christmas my true love sent to me
-a partridge in a pear tree
On the second day of Christmas my true love sent to me
-two turtle doves
On the third day of Christmas my true love sent to me
-three French hens
On the fourth day of Christmas my true love sent to me
-four Colley birds
On the fifth day of Christmas my true love sent to me
-five gold rings
On the sixth day of Christmas my true love sent to me
-six geese alaying
On the seventh day of Christmas my true love sent to me
-seven swans a swimming
On the eighth day of Christmas my true love sent to me

-eight maids a milking
On the ninth day of Christmas my true love sent to me
-nine drummers drumming
On the tenth day of Christmas my true love sent to me
-ten pipers piping
On the eleventh day of Christmas my true love sent to me
-eleven ladies dancing
On the twelfth day of Christmas my true love sent to me
-twelve Lords aleaping

PROLOGUE

He held them up; the gold sparkled as he dropped each one into the pot. One, two, three, four, five. In they went, barely making a splash. He stirred the soup quickly and walked out the door. "Now, I just have to wait."

CHAPTER 1

The fifth day of Christmas

The lights were dim in the large room. Each table was lit by candlelight. Christmas trees cast a glow upon the walls around the room. In the quiet atmosphere, the waiters moved throughout, not disturbing patrons.

Jeremy held up his glass of wine and said, "Here's to a nice Christmas as a family."

Emma held up her glass and clinked his. "I'm looking forward to it."

The waiter cleared his throat, signaling the food was ready. The soup Emma had ordered came at the same time as Jeremy's steak dinner. "You know, soup's not a meal," Jeremy said as he cut his steak.

"Sure, it is," she said and lifted the spoon to her mouth. Before it touched her lips, a scream bounced off the walls. Emma dropped her spoon and turned toward the woman making all the noise.

"OH MY GOD! There's a finger! IN MY SOUP!" the woman screamed.

Emma looked at Jeremy. "After you," he said and stood up. Emma followed him to the woman's table. Sure enough, a finger was in the bottom of the bowl, and it had a gold ring on it.

Emma called to the frozen waiter. "We need the manager, please."

A small man ran over and said in a hushed voice, "I'm the manager. What can I do for you?"

"First, you might take the bowl with a finger in it to the kitchen," she said drolly.

"Yes, of course, right away," the manager said, picking up the bowl. The finger floated to the top and he dropped it back on the table, causing the woman to scream again.

Jeremy said, "We're with the Pinkerton detectives. This will be a police matter."

Screams started to come from all sides of the restraint. Emma sighed. "And have the other bowls of soup picked up." The manager just stood there, staring at the finger bobbing in the bowl. She called to another waiter. "Please pick up all the soup and return it to the kitchen. We'll need to inspect it."

The man waved to the other waiters, and they moved to take the bowls back to the kitchen. The manager followed them, staring at the bowls. Emma started to follow and saw Jeremy had returned to their table. She walked over to him. "Would you like to join us?" she asked.

"Yeah, just a sec," he said. He went over, picked up his plate, and carried it to her. Emma raised her eyebrows as he lifted the fork with a slice of steak to his lips.

"What? They didn't find a finger in my food." He continued to eat as they entered the brightly lit kitchen.

The manager found his voice as he entered the kitchen. "Everyone, stop work!" he called.

The chef ran over, waving a knife. "Don't listen to him! Get

4

back to work." He turned back to them. "All of you, out! You have nothing to do with my kitchen." He looked at the waiters entering the doorway carrying trays. "Why is all of this soup being sent back?"

Emma got between the chef and the servers and stared him down. "Unless you intentionally served fingers to the guests, I think someone tampered with your soup."

"Fingers!" The chef waved to one of the servers. "Bring that here." The server took the bowl over and the chef stirred it with a spoon. The chef saw a finger bob to the top and stopped abruptly. "What do you need?"

"First, we'll need a runner to notify the police," Jeremy said.

"Our patrolman is usually down the block," volunteered a waiter, standing by the entrance to the dining room.

"Great." Jeremy reached out to Emma's pocket, took her notebook, and documented what was happening. "Get this to him. We'll wait here." The server ran off to deliver his note.

"Where's the soup?" asked Emma.

The chef waved to a large pot sitting on the burner. "There."

Jeremy told the waiters, "Line the soup up for us on this counter." The counter was a long prep counter; the assistant chefs stepped back to allow them room. They put the bowls down side-by-side. "Emma, you go check the pot. I'll check these."

Emma nodded and motioned to the head chef. "With me."

The man followed her to the large pot.

Jeremy examined each bowl; he moved the thick broth with a spoon. "This might be easier with a strainer."

"Right here, sir," called an assistant chef, holding one up.

"Good idea," called the chef. "Put a pot underneath it in case they need the liquids."

"Yes, chef." The assistant moved to set up the strainer and pot.

Jeremy waved to the servers. "Take a bowl, please." They

NOTEBOOK MYSTERIES ~ THE TWELVE DAYS OF MURDER

took the bowls to the sink and poured them into the sink. "Three fingers and three rings," Jeremy called to Emma.

She used a handheld strainer to drag through the soup. "Count that as five rings total and a hand over here."

"No other parts?"

"Not that I can find."

"Chef, who had access to this soup?" asked Emma.

He rubbed his neck. "Waiters, other chefs, managers."

The manager contributed to the list. "The soup cooks all day, so also delivery men."

The assistant chef who'd helped with the strainer spoke. "There was also a repair man."

The manager frowned. "I wasn't notified."

"He just said he was called to check under the sink."

"Did you stay with him?" the chef asked.

"No, sir, I was preparing the greens for the evening meal."

"We'll collect statements from everyone," Emma murmured. "We'll need to lock this place down."

Jeremy walked to the manager and spoke low in his ear. "Yes, I'll make an announcement," the man said.

"I'll come with you," said Jeremy.

The manager stopped and turned to the waiters. "Please, turn up the gas lights." The men moved quickly to follow his directions.

The people in the room had moved from their tables and stood in groups on the far side of the dining room. A man rushed over from one of the groups. "Can we leave? My wife is very upset."

Jeremy took over and said, "We'll need you to stay here until the police arrive. Statements will be taken from everyone."

The man nodded and moved back to the group. There were grumbles but the patrons stayed in the same place.

"What now?" asked the manager.

"Now, we wait."

In the kitchen, Emma looked at the chef. "I think the restaurant will be closed for tonight."

"You're right." He turned to his staff. "Turn off the burners and step back from the counters."

They followed his direction and waited. A short time later, the men in blue pushed into the restaurant. "Who's in charge here?" called out an officer from the door. Jeremy recognized him as Bill Coleman.

Jeremy walked over. "Bill, I see you got my note."

"I did. How did you happen to be here?"

"Dinner," he said.

He sighed. "Tell me what is going on."

After Jeremy went over the events, Bill directed his men. "These people don't want to stay here all night. Each of you, take a group, get names, addresses, and what they may have seen."

"Then can we go home?" asked a tall woman leaning on a much smaller man.

"Yes, as long as you cooperate, we should be able to get everyone out of here." The officers did as they were asked and started taking statements.

Bill looked over at Jeremy. "And where's Emma?"

Jeremy cocked his head toward the door behind him. "Kitchen."

"And where are the fingers located?"

"Come with me." Bill followed Jeremy into the kitchen. Jeremy pushed the door open, and Emma walked over to them.

"Bill, good to see you."

"Wish it was under different circumstances," he commented. "Where are the fingers?"

"In the sink, in a strainer."

The trio moved over to it and Bill said, "As reported, five fingers and a hand." He looked at Emma. "Any other body parts?"

"No, we went through the whole pot and only found those."

"What about the rest of the food?"

"We didn't find anything else," said Emma, gesturing to the man on her right. "This is Chef Chris. It's his kitchen."

Bill walked over to the chef. "We appreciate your help with this. We'll need statements from you and your staff."

"Whatever you need."

"The kitchen staff will need to be interviewed in the main dining room." They followed his direction and the kitchen went quiet. Bill walked over to Emma and Jeremy. "We'd like you to come down to the precinct."

"So much for a quiet night out," Jeremy muttered.

"At least you got to eat," she said, looking around the space.

"You're humming," he murmured.

"Am I? I didn't notice."

CHAPTER 2

Bill transported Emma and Jeremy, along with the fingers and hand, back to the precinct. Bill pointed. "I think you might join us in our planning room. It's over there."

Emma and Jeremy went into the room. She stopped at the door and frowned. The room was set up with rows of chairs and an aisle running to the front of the room. At the far wall, a pinboard stood. "Jeremy is this part of something bigger?" she said, walking over to the board and turning it to face them.

"Hey, stop that!" yelled an officer who was sitting in the room. "Don't touch that!"

Police Chief Robert Wilson McClaughry stood by the door. "Officer Davies, let her work."

The man jumped and turned toward him. "Sir, I didn't see you there." The chief gave the young man a long stare. "Yes, sir," Davies muttered as he slumped back into his chair.

Emma and Jeremy turned their attention back to the board. The board had a sign on it: **Ongoing events**.

"You're humming again," Jeremy said, looking at the board.

"Hmm," she said noncommittally, concentrating on the pictures in front of her.

"Got a real sick bastard out there," Jeremy noted.

"No," she said. "It's more than that." Emma moved closer to the board to read the notes under the pictures. "This is the wrong order." She started to move the pictures around.

"Hey!" Davies called again.

"Davies," McClaughry warned.

"But, but… she's ruining it," Davies complained, waving at Emma.

The chief ignored the officer and walked over to join them at the board. "Emma, tell us what we're missing," he said.

She continued to rearrange the pictures, ripping a page out of her notebook to be used as a placeholder for the five fingers, and stepped back. "Don't you see it?"

"See what?" Davies whined. "I just see you're messing up everything."

The trio ignored him. Jeremy tried to see what she did. "Ah, I'm not seeing it. You'll have to tell me."

Emma pointed to the first picture. "It was the head found in a tree that cinched it for me."

Davies moved up behind them.

"How are these related and why do you think that one was first?" asked Jeremy.

She started at the last picture and sang, "Five golden rings, four Colley birds, three French hens." Jeremy joined her at, "Two turtle doves and a partridge in a pear tree."

Davies frowned and narrowed his eyes at the pictures. "I see it all now. But the first one, how is that a partridge?"

"Look at his name," she suggested.

Jeremy leaned in and read, "Partridge. Like I said, a sick bastard."

"We have to stop him before he gets to six through twelve," said the chief.

Emma and Jeremy continued to study the board. Emma

sighed. "Christmas. There's so many better things to do. String popcorn..."

Jeremy continued, "Bake cookies, decorate trees..."

"Six geese a-laying is next. How do you look for something like that?" Emma asked, "Where were each of these found?" Jeremy asked, turning to the two men.

"We marked the map there," said Davies, walking to the large picture, on the wall. "A pin indicates each location where the bodies were found."

"Did you find any correlations?"

"We were under the assumption it was random," the officer admitted. The chief walked over to the door and called, "Bill." The man joined him. "Come in here. We need everyone to evaluate the new information."

Bill walked in and they briefed him on their suspicions.

"The grouping of pins is in this area. Why?" Emma asked, drumming her fingers on her lips.

"The murderer's familiar with the area?" suggested Bill.

As they studied the map, Jeremy looked at his watch. "Babe, we need to get home."

"We do," Emma said, continuing to study the map.

McClaughry said, "Emma, I'd like you and Jeremy to come in and meet with the rest of the task force. The team's been together since the second body turned up."

"What time?" Jeremy asked.

Bill took over from there, as he was the team leader. "Nine in the morning. We need to use the new information you provided to redirect the investigation."

"We'll be here," Jeremy confirmed. He held out his hand and Emma took it.

"No one is to be told of these events until we have an idea of what's going on," Bill commanded.

The duo nodded their agreement. "Of course," Emma agreed.

"Davies, can you ensure Emma and Jeremy get home?" Bill asked.

"Yes, sir." Emma and Jeremy accompanied the officer out of the room.

CHAPTER 3

ora sat in the sitting room reading. The Christmas tree ornaments glittered in the room, lit by low gas lights hanging on the walls. She heard the door creak open in the foyer. "Need to oil those hinges," Dora murmured.

Emma and Jeremy entered the house and removed their coats and hats. The lights drew them into the sitting room. "You're still up?" Emma asked her sister as she pushed her hair back from her face.

"Just winding down. How was dinner?"

"It was good," said Jeremy.

"Interesting," Emma replied. Dora put down her book with a frown. Emma spoke low in Jeremy's ear.

"Sure, just a second." Jeremy went to the kitchen.

"Care to explain the interesting comment?" Dora asked her sister.

"Not right now," Emma said, stifling a yawn. "It's been a long night." Jeremy returned and tossed an apple toward her; she caught it deftly. She took a big bite and said, "We'll see you in the morning."

Dora watched them go up the stairs. She picked up her book and stared at the pages, not comprehending the words.

"Hey," Tim called from the doorway. "Coming to bed?" She put down her book slowly and stood. "Something wrong?" he asked.

"Hmm, why an apple?" Dora muttered to herself.

"Apple? What apple?"

"Oh, just something I saw," she said and walked to her husband.

He pulled her close and looked up. "I see mistletoe." He grinned at her.

"Well, don't let it go to waste," Dora murmured. He didn't and lowered his head to hers. They had an enjoyable moment.

"Ready to go upstairs?" he asked.

She nodded and walked with him upstairs. "You were saying something about an apple?" he asked. "Is it apple pie? Or apple tarts? Or maybe Apfelkuchen?"

"I can't remember," she said with a laugh. His laugh joined hers.

CHAPTER 4

The sixth day of Christmas

The next morning, the table at the boarding house was full of lively talk of Christmas parties, baking, and children's activities.

Emma stopped at the foot of the stairs. "What're we going to tell them?"

"You heard Bill last night. This is to be kept quiet."

"You know that always gets me into trouble with this group."

"We can give them a few facts."

"Breakfast," Dora called out.

"We're coming in," Emma replied. She looked at Jeremy. "Ready?"

"After you."

They entered the dining room; the table was filled with breakfast platters and milk pitchers. They sat down and quickly filled their plates. Dora let Emma get a mouth full of a biscuit before she asked, "What happened last night?"

Emma choked and Jeremy pounded on her back. When she

finally drew a breath, she asked innocently, "What makes you think something happened?"

"There was that apple Jeremy got you."

"You think something happened because I ate an apple?" Emma delayed her answer.

"Oh, please," Dora scoffed. "I know you both. Something always happens to the two of you."

"Well…" Emma stammered

"You might want to answer her, Aunt Emma," her twelve-year-old nephew Patrick said. "You know she'll get it out of you."

"Careful," muttered Jeremy.

"I'll do my best." Emma looked around the table. "We're working with the police on a task force."

"Task force?" Tim asked, instantly alert. "How big is this?"

"We can't say, we just got involved last night."

"Will you keep us informed?" asked Dora.

"As much as we're allowed."

They finished breakfast. Dora continued to stare at them but didn't ask any more questions. After they exited the front door, Tim said, "Hey, you can't be mad at them keeping secrets. You know the kind of work they do. And, besides, you have secrets of your own."

"I know," she sighed. "I guess all will be revealed soon."

~

Jeremy and Emma stood outside, bracing themselves against the cold wind.

"Well, that went pretty well," said Jeremy as he waved to a cab.

"They know if we're working with police then we can't share as easily."

A covered carriage pulled up. "Where to, sir?" asked the

NOTEBOOK MYSTERIES ~ THE TWELVE DAYS OF MURDER

driver. Jeremy gave him the address to their parents' home, and they climbed in.

"Are we getting Cole involved?" she asked.

"We might need the extra manpower if you're right about the song."

"I am," she interrupted.

"Then we have another murder tonight."

"Six geese a-laying. How do we approach this one?"

"No idea, but I think we should involve as many people as possible."

"And we get to see Henrietta."

"A bonus." He grinned.

"Have you ordered the gift?"

He gave her a side look. "You know I have."

"Will it get here on time?"

"It will," he assured her. She laid her head on his shoulder and enjoyed the movement of the cab. "We're here," said Jeremy as they pulled to a stop.

"Ugh, back out into the cold. Why's it always so cold?"

"It is winter in Chicago," he pointed out.

"We might need to go somewhere warmer."

"Next case," he promised.

He paid the driver, and they ran up the stoop to the door. He knocked quickly and the door was swung open by Henrietta.

"Jeremy! Emma!"

"Hiya, Hen," Jeremy said, hugging the girl.

Emma hugged and kissed the top of the girl's head. "Have you had fun?"

"Yes, we're going Christmas shopping today."

"Let them in, Henrietta," called Abbey. "You're letting in the cold air!"

"Of course." Hen stepped back and let them in. They took off their coats, hats, and scarves. Abbey joined them, taking their winter things, and kissed Emma on the cheek. She moved the items to the closet, then returned to Jeremy and took his arm.

"You're here early; would you like some breakfast?"

"Dora took care of us," Emma told her stepmother.

"I wouldn't turn down a cup of coffee," Jeremy told her.

"Come into the dining room," Abbey said, turning gracefully, her skirt swishing on the marble floors. She led them to the room across the foyer.

"Morning, Ellis," Jeremy said as they entered.

"Morning, Papa," Emma told her father. She went to kiss him on the cheek.

He lowered his newspaper and peered at her over the top of his glasses. "Morning, little girl."

"Is Pops around?" Jeremy asked.

"I am," Cole called from the doorway. "Are you two going into the station now?"

Jeremy looked at Emma and she shrugged. "All right, what do you know?" Jeremy asked his father.

"I was contacted by Chief McClaughry last night. He indicated he already had you both on the team."

"What's the new case?" Henrietta asked.

Emma took the girl's hand. "This is a police matter. We'll share when we're allowed."

"Okay," Hen said and moved to sit at the table.

"Do I have time to eat?" Cole asked.

Jeremy checked his watch. "We have time. We need to be there by nine."

"Then I'll eat quickly." Cole walked to the side buffet and filled his plate.

They talked about the Christmas Day events and, when Cole finished, he said, "I'll get my coat. Meet me in the foyer?"

"We'll be ready."

"Should we be worried about anything?" Abbey asked.

"Not yet. If that changes, we'll let you know," Jeremy promised.

Emma hugged Hen. "We'll see you at home tomorrow."

"See you."

Jeremy walked over and kissed her on the head.

"I'll walk you out," Abbey said. Hen stayed with Ellis and they moved into the foyer. "Don't put yourself in unnecessary danger," she said to the duo.

Jeremy got their winter things and tossed Emma's at her. She caught it and pulled on her coat. She wrapped her scarf around her neck and pulled on her hat. "All set."

Jeremy had done the same. Cole came down the stairs, buttoning up his black suit jacket. "Let's go."

"Coat and hat, Cole," reminded Abbey.

He looked out the window. "Ah, winter in Chicago." He got his coat, hat, and scarf.

"Hey, the carriage is already outside," Jeremy said, glancing out the window.

"I ordered it earlier," Cole told his son.

The three headed out into the cold snowy morning. They huddled down into their coats and walked quickly to the carriage. Cole gave the address to the driver and joined them inside. "I understand you had a surprise in your soup," Cole stated.

"Not me. I had the steak," said Jeremy.

"Jeremy avoided the soup." Emma lowered her voice in an approximation of a man's voice. "Soup's not a meal, you know."

"I don't sound like that," Jeremy said.

"I don't sound like that," Emma continued in a low voice.

"Cut it out," Jeremy complained.

"Cut it out," Emma mocked him.

"Pops," Jeremy whined, "Emma's making fun of me. Make her stop."

"I swear, sometimes you two are worse than children," Cole lamented.

"He means you, Jeremy." Emma smiled at him sweetly.

"He does not."

"He does, too."

"Does not."

"Does, too."

Cole was used to their banter and waited patiently. "Tell me about fingers," he finally prompted.

Emma grimaced. "Yeah, it didn't occur to me that this was related to the song until I saw all the four other murders on that board."

"Any ideas on the next one?"

"Well, day six is six geese a-laying," she said.

"It's winter. I'm not sure where geese could be found," said Jeremy.

Cole thought about it and said, "The Lincoln Park Zoo."

"It's been open for a couple of years," Emma said. "I haven't had a chance to go there."

"Me either. Maybe we should take Hen there," said Jeremy.

"When it's warmer," agreed Emma.

"Who runs the place?" Jeremy asked his father.

"The director is Cy DeVry," said Cole.

"I've heard of him, kind of a flamboyant man," Emma said, thinking of what she'd read about him.

"He is that," Cole agreed. "The zoo's become a rather big attraction now. I think it started with elephants and monkeys. Now, it's gotten much bigger since."

They thought about that as the carriage made its way through the snow to the precinct. Once there, the three hurried into the building. Emma and Jeremy led the way to the meeting room. It was already full of officers, filling chairs on both sides of the aisles. The three took seats in the back.

"We have an update," Bill started as he walked to the bulletin board and turned it around.

"Sir," a young officer in the front of the room said, "has someone moved the order of the pictures? It's not in the order we found the bodies."

Coleman acknowledged the officer with a nod of his head. "We have some consultants with us today, Emma Evans, Cole, and Jeremy Tilden from the Pinkertons. Emma, would you like to come up here and tell the group your theory and why the pictures were moved?"

Emma stood and went to the front of the room. She nodded at the officer who had voiced the question. "I did change the order because of the scene Jeremy, and I witnessed last night. We were at Michael's Steak House when we found five fingers with five golden rings."

The silence broke out into multiple conversations overlapping. A baritone sang out, "Five golden rings." She pointed to the last picture on the board. "Four Colley birds." The macabre picture showed a dead woman with the four birds made into a necklace. "Three French hens." She moved to the grouping of three women tied up and tortured. "Two turtle doves?" A man and woman clutching two birds. "And a partridge in a pear tree."

"I don't see a bird for the first one," commented an older officer, Charles Williams.

Emma explained. "His name was Partridge."

"And his head was found in a pear tree. We found him in a private garden," Williams stated.

Jeremy joined Emma and asked, "Was the garden connected to the case in any special way?"

"No, the owner's been on vacation in Europe for the past three months," Bill replied.

"It may be that was the only pear tree in that area," suggested Emma.

"It's odd," Williams said. "Whoever's doing this seems ignorant of the fact that the twelve days of Christmas starts on Christmas Day, not twelve days before." There were nods throughout the room.

Coleman walked toward Emma and took over. "That doesn't change the fact he's using this song to commit murder. So far, there seems to be no connection to the people except for the areas they were found in." He went to the map and tapped it. He turned to continue when a young officer entered the room.

"Sir!" the office called out. Coleman ignored him. "Sir," he said again.

Bill sighed and gave him his full attention. "Yes."

"Mr. DeVry from the Lincoln Park Zoo is here; he wants to speak with you about a theft."

Cole stood and said, "I contacted him this morning with an inquiry about missing geese."

Bill slowly nodded. "Okay, show him in. Wait, let's get that board turned around. Help me, Charlie." Bill and Williams turned the board and then waited for DeVry to enter. The officer accompanied a large man with a heavy mustache, a stub of a lit cigar in his mouth.

"Is that a tooth on his necklace?" Emma asked in a low voice.

Jeremy looked at the man. "Looks like."

"You had something to tell us?" Coleman asked.

"After I received Mr. Tilden's note, I confirmed we had a theft last night. Some animals were taken," said Mr. DeVry in a loud, booming voice.

"Which ones?" asked Emma.

"Six geese, seven swans, and a cow."

Six, seven, and eight! Emma thought as she nudged Jeremy. He nodded in acknowledgment.

"I'm worried that these animals will die if they aren't cared for properly," DeVry said. "What're you going to do about it? Will you assign some officers to find them?"

"We will," Coleman assured the man. "Can you give all the

details to Officer Johnson?" He motioned to the officer on his right.

Johnson stood and said, "Follow me, sir."

They waited for the duo to leave and closed the door firmly behind them. "Board," Coleman directed. This time, Emma and Jeremy turned it to the group. Bill reviewed the board. "It looks like the song and murders will continue. Any suggestions on where to start?"

Emma walked over to the area where the murders were grouped on the map. "I'd suggest we look for locations where the animals could be held in this area."

Groans went out through the room. Williams spoke up for the group. "Ma'am, that's overwhelming. They could be anywhere: basements, storerooms, even apartments."

Chief McClaughry stepped into the back of the room and quietly shut the door. His voice rang out. "We must protect our citizens."

Bill stepped up. "Sir, we'll send out teams throughout that part of town."

"I don't think so," Cole said.

"Do you have something to suggest?" Coleman asked. His patience was waning with these consultants.

"I do. I think that you should use the officers who normally walk the beat. You can add to them, but these officers are known to the residents in these areas and are trusted. The residents may be more willing to answer their questions."

"Good idea," McClaughry responded from the back of the room.

Bill nodded begrudgingly. "We'll do that, but we'll add extra men."

"We'll help," Jeremy said.

"No," Emma insisted, "we might be more helpful here." She continued to study the board.

Jeremy quirked an eyebrow at her. "Then we stay," he acquiesced.

"Good," the chief replied. "Bill, I leave this with you to organize. Keep me informed of your progress."

"Yes, sir."

"Gentlemen and lady." McClaughry nodded his head at Emma and left the room. She acknowledged his response with a nod of her head.

Bill spoke to the group. "We'll keep the details under wraps. We're only looking for noise complaints or animal sounds at this time."

"And missing persons?" asked one of the officers.

"Yes, if anyone is missing, report back here immediately."

The men nodded and headed out.

Coleman called, "Williams, we'll be running two shifts and, if anyone wants extra hours, we have it."

"Yes, sir."

Coleman gathered his things and headed out.

Emma hadn't moved. She tapped her fingers on her lips, studying the pictures.

"Got any ideas?" Jeremy asked her.

"Just thinking ahead. There's seven more days of murder left."

"If we don't catch him first."

"We have to. This can't go on."

Cole walked over. "There isn't much that can be done now," he told the duo. "We have to let the police do their jobs and report back."

"Hmm," Emma pondered. "You're right. We wait."

"While we wait," Jeremy put in, "we have some shopping to do."

She smiled. "You know, you're right."

Cole knew them and remarked, "Try to stay out of trouble."

"Us?" Jeremy asked. "Pops, relax. We're just going Christmas shopping."

"Then I'm in need of a new watch."

"Noted."

"We have a few names on the list," Emma said innocently. "We still need something for Amy also."

Cole frowned at her. "Just stay out of trouble." He walked out of the room, his head hung down.

Jeremy sat on the edge of the desk. "What was that about Amy?"

"Oh, nothing. I'm just thinking about what we still need to buy." He frowned at her, looking very similar to Cole at that moment. She reached up and smoothed the lines. "We should be going soon."

"Sure."

They exited the station and caught the first carriage that went by. He gave the driver the address; it was a store located in the middle of the murder area.

"Not going to get into trouble?" Emma asked, smiling.

"Of course not. I think this store will have just the gifts you're looking for." The carriage pulled up to a store that carried an assortment of nice items. They went in. The store was quiet.

"We got here at the right time," she said, looking around at the filled shelves and multiple display cabinets.

"Let's look around."

The clerk behind the counter was counting receipts and nodded at them. They approached the long case; it held an assortment of gold and silver decorative items. The clerk walked up to them and Emma tapped the cabinet. "The combs, I'd like to see them, please." They were silver with an intricate design, shaped like a crown.

"Those look like wedding combs. Who are they for?" Jeremy asked as the clerk laid them on the counter.

"I was thinking of Amy."

Jeremy frowned. "Is she getting married? I didn't know she was seeing anyone."

"Hmm," she said noncommittally. "I think she'll like them."

"They are nice," he agreed, touching them.

"They are our best," the clerk remarked. "Would you like me to wrap them up?"

"Yes, please," Emma replied.

He pulled out a piece of brown paper and a box. The combs were moved into it, placed artfully, and the box closed.

Jeremy leaned on the counter. "Have you heard any rumors of anyone being hurt in the area?"

The man's hands stilled. "Why would you ask that?"

"We had friends tell us to be careful while we were shopping."

"Oh, well," the clerk responded, wrapping the box in the brown paper and using twine to secure it, "yes. That's why we're closing early." He waved toward the sign on the door; it indicated that the store would be closing at three pm.

"A boy who used to work for me and the jeweler across the street warned us to get home early." The bell rang above the door and another couple walked in. "I'll be right with you," the clerk called to them. He turned back to Emma and Jeremy and smiled. "Why don't we get this transaction completed?"

"Of course." Jeremy paid the man, took the box, and placed it into his coat. As the clerk moved toward the other couple, Emma murmured, "I think we should look over at the jewelers for that watch."

"That's right, Pops mentioned he needed one."

He offered her his elbow and Emma took it, saying "Thank you" over her shoulder. The clerk at the counter waved at them. They crossed the street and entered the jewelry store. There were several people browsing. "I'll be right with you," a dapper man in a blue suit and gray hair called.

"Thank you," Jeremy called back. "Watches?" The man pointed to the cabinet to his right. Emma and Jeremy strolled over and looked at each one.

"Any idea which one he might like?" Emma asked, glancing down at the selection.

"I'm not sure. Silver or gold?"

"Hmm. Gold, I think." Emma nodded, examining each one.

The clerk completed the sale and, when the other couple was ready, he moved to them. "Would you like to see one of the watches?"

"We would," Emma replied.

"Anything in particular or a selection?"

Emma tapped the glass. "This one, please."

The clerk smiled. "That is a nice choice. It's a stunning 9K gold H. Huguenin Locle and is numbered on the back here." He flipped it over for her to see.

"The details are quite amazing," Emma remarked as he handed her the watch.

"Is that a ship?" Jeremy inquired, examining it closely.

"Yes, the artistry is amazing," the clerk replied.

"It reminds me of Pop's and Mom's, just before they were married. Do you think he'll like it?" Jeremy asked Emma.

"I think he'll love it, but you probably shouldn't bring that up around Papa," she teased. Her papa had married Jeremy's mom long after Cole and she had divorced.

"You're right. I still think he'll like it."

"So do I; we'll take it."

Jeremy started to pull out his wallet, but Emma stopped him. "No, I'll get this one. You got the combs."

He shrugged. The clerk wrapped the watch in the same way the clerk in the last store had wrapped the combs. Jeremy leaned close to the clerk. "The clerk across the way mentioned you were given some advice to close early."

NOTEBOOK MYSTERIES ~ THE TWELVE DAYS OF MURDER

"Yes," the clerk acknowledged in a low voice, "we were told it might be dangerous to be outside after three pm."

"Who mentioned it?" Emma queried.

"A kid who used to work for me and Greg, the clerk across the street. He was concerned about us." The other couple called over to him. He turned to leave and then turned back to Emma and Jeremy. "You'd best not be in the street in the evenings. All the stores in this area are closing early."

"Jeremy," Emma told him, "we have a lot of shopping to finish."

"You're right. Thank you, Mr.—"

"Wilson. Merry Christmas."

"You, too," Emma replied as they headed out.

"Who else do we have to buy for?" Jeremy wondered aloud.

"Well, we have Dora's art set, Abbey's dress… Oh, Papa's gramophone arrived last week."

"We now have Amy's and Pop's gifts. What's left?"

"We still have Hen."

"I need some small things, and we need to pick up her dresses."

"So, who's left? The kids and Tim?"

She checked the time again. "We need to get going if we want to finish the list before the stores close."

They hurried out of the shop.

CHAPTER 5

ℰ

*M*ark Sutherland lay on top of his bedcovers, staring at the ceiling, when he heard a knock. He looked toward the door but, when the second knock came, he turned toward the window. There was only one person that could be. He went to it and opened the sash. Enzo Marella stood there grinning at him. "Well, come on in. I don't know why you can't just use the front door," Mark told him. Enzo was his best friend who seemed to keep him in trouble.

"What fun would there be in that?" Enzo asked as he climbed into the room.

Mark checked the clock. "What're you doing out so late?"

His friend shrugged and walked around the room, picking up random objects. "It's not so late. I just had to get out of the house." He took off his coat and threw it on the floor. "All the parents talk about are babies, and they're always at the house. I just had to get away. With Christmas, everyone is there."

"Do they know you're gone?"

"I left a note and told them I'd be over here." A baby's cry sounded. "What is that?" Enzo screeched, covering his ears with his hands.

Mark listened. "Sounds like a baby to me."

"A baby? I thought I'd get away from that here. When did a baby move in?"

"The baby didn't move in by itself, genius. It's a grandmother and a little girl. They arrived a few days ago and I think they're staying through Christmas."

The crying continued and Enzo's mouth tightened. "Want to get out of here?"

Mark frowned at the clock; it was nine pm. "What're you thinking?"

"Anywhere I can get away from that damn noise!"

Mark shrugged. "Sure, why not?" He sat up to pull on his shoes and his sweater. Enzo was already half out the window.

"Hey, we can use the door," Mark commented.

"You want to be seen?"

"Well, yes, my parents trust me."

Enzo pulled in his leg and closed the window. "Fine, if you say so," he replied doubtfully.

"I do say so." Mark grabbed his hat, coat, and gloves. He gestured to the coat Enzo had thrown on the floor. "You gonna bring that?"

"Nah, I get too hot in it."

"It is winter in Chicago," Mark pointed out and waited.

"Fine, *Mom*, I'll take it with me, but you can't make me wear it."

"Don't be surprised if you end up wearing it before we leave the house." Enzo shot Mark a dirty look. Mark held up his hands in surrender. "I'm just sayin'."

Enzo frowned at him as he followed his friend downstairs. There was a conversation ongoing in the dining room. The boys entered and found Mark's mom and dad sitting at the table playing cards.

"Enzo! Are you visiting?" Elizabeth, Mark's mother, asked.

"Yes, ma'am."

"There's lots of people in his house right now," Mark explained to his parents.

"Lots of babies," muttered Enzo under his breath.

George, Mark's father, looked toward the stairs. "Us, too."

"Oh, she'll calm down soon. She just gets upset at bedtime," Elizabeth said. "Mark was the same way." She grinned at Mark.

"*MOM!* Not in front of my friends," Mark pleaded. Elizabeth blew him a kiss.

"Until she calms down, we play cards. You boys want me to deal you in?" George asked the boys.

"Enzo wants to go for a walk."

"The weather's clear right now, but it's still cold. You two have on long johns?" Elizabeth asked. Mark and Enzo nodded. "Coats and gloves?"

"Check and check," confirmed Mark.

Elizabeth looked pointedly at Enzo's coat, which was draped over his arm. "And you, Enzo? Put on your coat."

The boy knew better than to argue. "Yes, ma'am," he said, pulling it on.

"Muffler also," she commented. He mumbled and put it around his neck. She nodded her approval.

George looked down at his cards. "Don't stay out too late."

"We won't," Enzo said. "Let's go." He grabbed Mark's sleeve and pulled him out the door.

"Hopefully we'll be in bed when you get home," George said with another long glance upstairs.

The boys waved and left the house. Enzo started to stride away determinedly.

"Hey," Mark called, "wait for me. Where are you going in such a hurry? I thought you just wanted to go outside."

"I did, but I found something last night I thought you might be interested in."

Mark nodded and kept pace with his friend. After a while,

Mark asked, "Just how far is this thing?" Enzo mumbled something. "What was that?"

"The warehouses by the water."

"Hold it." Mark stopped Enzo, grabbing him by the sleeve. "Why were you over there? That area's dangerous."

"I was just hanging out."

"With no reason?" Mark asked suspiciously. Enzo looked away, avoiding his direct gaze. "Well?" he asked expectantly.

"I was following someone." Mark stared and waited. Enzo squirmed. "I was working at that older house with Papa. I'd finished and was outside loading the wagon. Another wagon drove past and nearly hit me."

"So, you went after him?"

"Not exactly. Something was coming out of the back of the wagon. So, I followed."

"On foot?" Mark asked skeptically.

"They were going slow."

"What was it?"

"Let me show you?" Enzo implored. He waved his hand toward his friend to move him along. They walked the many blocks to the warehouse area. "Over there," he indicated and climbed up on a trash container and held out his hand to Mark. Mark took it and Enzo pulled him up.

"Right here." Enzo pointed out a small section of the window that he'd cleaned on his last visit.

Mark went over and looked in. "What am I looking at?"

"Give it a minute."

Mark heard something and asked, "What was that?"

"There." Enzo pointed.

"What is that? Swans?" Mark's voice was incredulous.

"And geese."

"But why are they here?"

"I'm not sure, but I'm concerned about them being kept locked up in here. Why are they here? Are they warm enough and are they being taken care of?"

"And where did they come from?"

"I don't know. Should we call someone?" asked Enzo.

"No, it may just be... Wait, something is going on."

"What?" Enzo moved back to look through the glass. "They seem to be gathering up the geese and putting them into crates."

"That's good; maybe they're going to their final home."

Enzo's mouth was drawn down. "I'm not so sure. These guys aren't very good with them. Watch how they're just pushing the birds into the crates."

"We can watch them and see where they're going," Mark suggested.

"Yeah, that would be good." Enzo rubbed his head, dislodging his hat. Mark caught it and held it while Enzo looked around. "I see the wagon they're using. Let's head over there. Maybe we'll hear something."

Mark shoved the hat back onto Enzo's head. "Just don't get us into trouble."

"I won't," he promised.

The horse and wagon were parked outside the warehouse door. They got to the far side of the wagon as the doors started to slide open. The boys dropped low and hid in the front of the wagon. "We gotta get these birds to Bughouse Square Park," the first man said as they loaded a container into the wagon. "Come on, Griff," he called to the other man, "we have a lot to move." They went back into the building.

"Bughouse Square," Mark whispered. "That's a good thing. It has three acres and a fountain."

"In winter?" Enzo challenged. "They need to be protected from the cold, not released to die."

"You're right," Mark admitted. "Once they drop them off, we can see about getting them moved someplace safe."

"You think so?" Enzo asked hopefully.

"Yeah. Let's head over there and wait for them."

Enzo stopped him. "Wait, they're coming out again." They dropped back down and watched the men.

The men exited, carrying another crate. "I'm worried about the boss, Griff; he seems to like his part of the plan a bit too much," the first man complained.

"Keep your eyes on the prize, Reed," Griff advised.

"Yeah, yeah." Reed sneezed. "I'll be glad to get rid of these animals."

"Just seven more days," Griff told him. The duo headed back into the warehouse.

"What do you think they meant by that?" Enzo asked his friend.

"I'm not sure." Mark looked at the wagon. "You know, it might be easier to ride with them."

"You're right. It beats walking," Enzo agreed. He started to climb in the wagon.

"Let's wait for them to leave," Mark advised.

Reed and Griff continued to complain as they loaded two geese and went back to the warehouse. The boys quickly slid behind the two geese. They squawked at them as they crawled under a blanket and stayed still.

"The birds are loud tonight," Griff growled, loading another set of geese.

"They're always loud," Reed fumed.

"Come on, I want to get this done. We have to do it before midnight."

"All right, all right, don't get your knickers in a knot," Reed groused.

Midnight, thought Mark. *What's going to happen at midnight?*

"I haven't heard anything in the paper," Griff asked. "Wasn't all this supposed to make a splash?"

"The boss says the quieter it is, the bigger it is."

"I guess that makes sense," Griff replied. The two men jumped onto the driver's seat, and the wagon started to move.

Enzo and Mark stayed quiet and tried not to move as the wood boxes began banging into them. The trip took time, the birds were settled, and the men continued talking.

"Any idea what the boss has set up?" questioned Griff.

"Nope, and I don't care. We just have to get to the Square and secure the birds." They drove in silence; the birds weren't moving.

"I see something," said Griff. "It looks like a nest and are those eggs?" he asked incredulously.

"Like I said, I don't care." Reed pulled the wagon to a stop and said, "Go over and see how we're going to keep the birds in place."

Griff jumped down and went over to the large nest. "There's some ropes here," he called back.

"Okay, come over and we'll secure the first one." A scraping sounded as they dragged the first container off.

"Now," said Mark. He and Enzo jumped out of the wagon and ran to a nearby tree to watch.

"That was close," Enzo panted.

"Yeah, any ideas on what they're doing?" Mark asked.

"I don't know. A Christmas display?"

"With geese?"

Enzo frowned. "Yeah, you're right. We need to get someone out here before those birds freeze."

Mark looked around. "We need to grab a cab."

"Got any money on you?" asked Enzo.

Mark turned to his friend. "You came out in the middle of the night with no money in your pockets?"

Enzo shrugged. "Spent most of my money on Christmas."

"Next time, plan ahead," ordered Mark.

"Yeah, well, I wasn't planning on jumping in the back of a wagon full of geese being driven by two guys to Bughouse Square for some ungodly reason," Enzo fumed at Mark. After a few minutes, the boy calmed down. "So, do you have any money?" he asked.

"Yeah, I do. Let's head that way." Mark waved to his left. "We should be able to get a cab closer to the restaurants."

Enzo followed him. "What about the police?"

"No, let's get Jeremy and Emma. They'll know what to do."

"Sounds like a plan."

As they wandered off, a man watching them stepped back into the shadow and rubbed his hands together. "Six geese a laying," he sang in a low voice.

"Hey, there's one," called Enzo. He ran after the carriage. He turned back to his lagging friend. "Well, come on!"

Mark hurried to keep pace with Enzo. They climbed in and gave the driver Emma's boarding house address.

"This has been a weird night," Mark commented.

"Yeah, it has," Enzo agreed. "But kinda fun." He grinned.

The carriage pulled up to the boarding house. Enzo jumped down and Mark followed. Mark paid the driver and asked, "Can you stay?"

"Jeez, kid, I don't know. It's cold out here. But I might do it for a price." Mark gave him some more money. He looked down at it. "I can stay."

They ran up to the front door and knocked. Tim opened the door. "What are you boys running around at this time of night for? And why do you have a carriage?"

Mark ignored the questions and asked, "Are Emma and Jeremy home?"

"Mark, what do you need?" Emma called from behind Tim.

Tim stepped back and let the boys into the foyer.

Mark rubbed his neck. "Can we talk in private?" he asked Emma.

"Sure." She waved to Jeremy to join them in the dining room.

"What is it?" Jeremy asked as he joined them.

"We found something odd at the park."

"Odd?" Emma looked at Jeremy. "Tell us."

"Geese…" Mark started.

"Geese?" Jeremy asked.

"Yeah. Six of them."

Emma interrupted with, "Where?"

"At Bughouse Park."

"Jeremy!" Emma exclaimed with wide eyes.

"Getting our coats out now," he said, walking quickly to the closet. He tossed Emma hers and they headed to the door.

"But we haven't told you what we need," Mark insisted

Emma put her hand to her lips and drummed them. "Jeremy, we need a carriage."

"We have one waiting," Enzo said.

"Good, let's go," Jeremy directed.

As they headed out, Tim called out, "What's happened?"

"We'll let you know later," Emma called back.

"Hang on a sec." Jeremy stopped them. "We need to get word to the police." He stopped and looked around. He ran to the side table in the dining room, got out some paper, scribbled a note, and handed it to Tim. "You need to notify the police and have them go to Bughouse Square as soon as possible. And don't mention this to anyone."

Dora went over to Tim and looked at the folded paper. "Have you read it?" she asked.

"No."

"There's more to this than what they're telling us, you know."

"We'll corner them tonight; right now, I need to get this to the police station." He followed the group out and ran down to where he could get a carriage.

Jeremy, Emma, Mark, and Enzo climbed into the waiting carriage. "Take us back to where you picked us up," Mark told the driver.

"Yes, sir." The driver started the carriage moving. The wind had lessened, and the night was clear. The driver took them to the location and dropped them off.

"Follow us," Mark said. He and Enzo started to stride toward the area where they'd left the men.

"Wait," called Emma, "we need to approach this quietly."

"It won't matter," Mark replied.

"Yeah, it's not gonna be quiet," muttered Enzo.

Emma frowned at him. "What do you mean?"

"You'll see."

The closer they got to the area, the louder the geese squawked. They looked around and, when they didn't see anyone nearby, they ran over to the nest.

"Poor girls," Enzo lamented. "They're freezing." Jeremy and Emma ignored him as they began examining the "eggs".

"Got any thoughts?" he asked.

"Just terrible ones," she said, looking at the size of the eggs.

"Could they have…" he asked, reaching toward one.

"Don't touch them," she warned.

"Too late, the geese must have cracked this one." Jeremy used her shoe to turn it over. A head rolled out. Emma jumped and glanced at the boys. They were occupied with the geese, trying to warm them up. "Cover it up," she muttered as she moved to block the view of the boys.

"With what?"

"Oh, for God's sake." She reached down and pulled off her heavy petticoat and draped it over the head.

"Did you find something?" asked Enzo, noticing the petticoat.

"Yeah," replied Emma.

"What was it?"

Mark turned toward them, waiting for the answer. "We'll tell you later," she said. The boys knew that look on her face and didn't ask any more questions.

"I think company's coming," Jeremy observed, looking down the road.

Wagons full of policemen rolled up.

"All this to help with the birds?" asked Enzo, impressed.

"Uh, yeah. That, too," said Emma.

Coleman ran over. "Is it another one?"

"What does it look like?" asked Emma. "We're sitting in a nest with six geese and eggs."

"That fits." He looked at the birds as the men piled up behind him.

"What first?" Davies asked. Coleman looked a bit at a loss.

"The birds. We need them carefully moved to a warm location," beseeched Enzo.

"Sir, we can put them in the wagon and move them to the horse barn until we can get them back to the zoo," volunteered Davies.

"Good idea."

"They've secured the animals with ropes, but we need to remove them one at a time and not disrupt the eggs," said Emma.

Everyone pitched in and the geese didn't fight the men; they were too cold. Once they were loaded into the closed-in wagon, Enzo asked, "Can Mark and I help get them settled?"

"Sure, come with us," Davies replied.

Jeremy said, "I'm glad they went with the geese."

"They don't need to experience this firsthand," she agreed.

"Well, what do we have here?" Coleman asked. She uncovered the head and the cracked "egg". He sighed. "Most likely each one is full of body parts."

Another wagon pulled up; Jake and additional officers piled out.

"Jake! I'm glad you're here," said Bill. "We'll want you over here."

He carried his camera over to them. "A nest and eggs. Any birds?"

"Yeah, they've been transported."

"I'm just glad we found them before they froze to death," said Jeremy.

"The timing didn't help the man," Jake said, picking up his camera. He moved around the nest and took pictures from different angles. He put the camera down. "I'm done." He looked around. "Does the fountain have significance?"

Emma looked at it. "I don't think so."

Bill said, "We need to get these to the coroner's office."

"How do we transfer these without breaking the remainder of the eggs?" Williams asked.

Emma examined the nest. "We can move the straw here and use it for padding." Everyone pitched in and got the wagon padded. They took their time with the eggs. When they got to the head, one of the officers asked, "Would you mind if we keep the petticoat to transport the head?"

"Yeah. I don't think I'm ever going to wear it again."

Once everything was in the wagon, the group transported them slowly to the police station. Emma and Jeremy sat with Jake in the back of the other wagon, and Bill and Williams drove the wagon. While they slowly followed, Bill turned and said, "Jake, we'll need you to take pictures at the coroner's office."

He nodded and sat quietly holding his camera. They stopped at the coroner's office to drop off the eggs. The process was handled slowly and carefully. After that, they made their way to the team room. The task force had started to assemble to discuss the latest murder.

The chief walked in and asked, "Another one?"

"Yes." Bill described the scene.

McClaughry turned to Emma. "How did you find it?"

"It wasn't us. It was two boys we know."

"Where're they now?"

"At the horse barn getting the geese settled until DeVry can be notified," Coleman replied.

"Geese! What geese?" the chief said. He'd been informed only of the murder.

"On the sixth day of Christmas, my true love gave to me, six geese a-laying," Jeremy sang.

"That's right." McClaughry turned to Bill. "Have the boys brought up immediately. We need answers."

Mark and Enzo were located and shown into a small interrogation room. "Are we in trouble?" Enzo asked nervously, looking around the room.

"No, I don't think so," Mark told his friend. At least, he hoped they weren't. When Emma and Jeremy walked into the room, Mark started to breathe again until he saw who followed. It was the chief of police and two other officers who'd been at the scene. Mark sat up straighter and Enzo followed his lead.

Emma and Jeremy sat, and the chief stood at the end of the table with two officers flanking him.

"Emma, why don't you start?" asked the chief.

"Enzo, Mark, tell us how you happened upon the nest tonight."

"Well…" Enzo hesitated.

"Just tell them. We won't get into trouble," Mark implored.

Enzo took a deep breath. "Last night, I noticed two men moving some geese, so I followed them. They took them to a warehouse at the dock."

"Just what were you expecting to find?" asked the chief.

"I wanted to make sure they weren't going to hurt the geese."

"Go on," encouraged Emma.

"I got Mark to go down and see them tonight."

"You saw the geese?" asked Emma.

Mark interrupted, "Well, it wasn't just geese. We saw swans also."

"And a cow," Enzo added.

"Where?" asked Jeremy, jumping to his feet. Enzo stuttered out the address. "We need to go now!"

McClaughry turned to Coleman. "Bill, get organized and head over to that warehouse. Take a full team."

"I'm going with you," Jeremy said. He looked at Emma. "You coming?"

"No, I need to go with Jake to the morgue for the breaking of the eggs."

"Jeremy, can we go with you?" asked Mark. He and Enzo had pulled on their coats and were waiting by the door.

"They did lead us to the latest scene," commented Emma.

"Okay, you can come, but you stay with me, and do as I say," Jeremy directed.

"We will," the boys promised.

Jeremy went over to Emma. "See you on the other side." He gave her a quick kiss and left the room.

Jake walked up to the door. "Ready?" she asked. He nodded and held up his camera. She walked with him down the hall. "Are you ready for this?"

"Part of the job. The eggs are weird."

"Yeah, they are." They continued outside to the waiting wagon that would take them to the coroner.

～

The group arrived at the warehouse. Coleman directed the men. "Williams, you take the back. Davies and I will take the front." He looked at Jeremy and the boys. "Once we clear the area, you can come in. Understood?"

"Understood," Jeremy answered for them. The men moved to their positions around the building and went in guns drawn.

"Hey, up here," Enzo called. He'd climbed to the spot where he'd seen the men inside the warehouse.

"What're you doing up there?" asked Jeremy, exasperated.

"It's the window where we were able to see what was happening," Mark explained.

"Well, what're we waiting for?" He and Mark joined Enzo. "What do you see?" he asked Enzo, squinting through the glass.

"The police are going in now," observed Mark.

"The two guys from earlier aren't there," said Enzo. "Can we go down now?"

"We wait until it's clear," Jeremy replied. They watched the scene below unfold. The officers moved in from the edges and across the large expanse. The door opened on the far side and swans came out.

"Can you see how many there are?" asked Enzo.

"Seven," muttered Jeremy.

"Yeah," said Mark. "How did you know that? You weren't looking."

"Just a guess," Jeremy said dryly. Mark looked at Enzo and he shrugged.

A voice called out. It was Davies. "Jeremy! The area's clear."

"On our way," Jeremy called back. The three jumped down and followed the officer back inside the building. Jeremy watched the men running after the swans. "Bill, there should be a cow, too."

"We haven't found her yet," Coleman admitted.

"We'll help you look," volunteered Enzo, and he ran off.

"Hey, wait for me," Mark called as he ran after his friend.

Both seven and eight, Jeremy thought. *Did we stop it or just delay it for another two days?*

∾

The coroner's office

. . .

An officer accompanied Emma and Jake as their driver. When they got to the coroner's office, he dropped them off and said, "I'll be back in an hour. Will that be long enough?"

Emma looked at Jake. "That should be fine," he acknowledged. The officer pulled away to take the horse back to a warm environment.

Jake and Emma went into the quiet building. An officer called down the hall to them. "Goldman is waiting for you. Lots to see."

"This way," Jake told Emma. She followed him down the long, narrow hallway. He turned and pushed the door open on his left. They entered a large room with tables, sheets covering the people lying on them.

"Over here, Jake," Goldman said. "I waited for you."

Emma determinedly followed Jake. The head they had found earlier had been hard enough, but she'd see this through. Jake walked over to the desk to get his film and camera organized. He turned back to them and approached the table.

"Are you ready?" asked the coroner.

"I'm ready."

Emma swallowed hard. "Me, too."

Goldman uncovered the eggs; the head had been moved to another table. Jake took a picture of the closed eggs and said, "You can open the first one now."

The coroner used a small hammer to crack into the first egg. "They're not geese eggs," he said. "They're far too thick. I think they're paper mâché." The first egg was emptied and chunks of body parts dropped onto the table.

"It's a meat puzzle," observed Emma.

"Yes," the coroner sighed, "looks like a long night for me."

After each egg was cracked open, the body pieces were moved to the table with the head. It took time to empty the rest of the eggs and move the parts to the other table. Goldman started to work with his macabre puzzle. He looked at Emma and Jake. "You might as well go home. I'll be working on this through the night."

Jake waved at Emma. "He wants to be alone with his work."

"Oh, okay. What next?"

"I'll develop the film, then head home."

"I'll wait for you," she promised.

"It'll be a while," he warned.

"That's okay. I need to review the board again," she replied, drumming her fingers on her lips

At the far end of the hall, the officer who dropped them off stepped inside the heavy outer door. He dusted the snow off his uniform. "We should get going; the snow's started again." They followed him quickly, buttoning up their coats and pulling on their hats. The ride back was mercifully short. Emma and Jake huddled together as they made their way up the stoop into the station. The officer pulled away, relieved that he and his horses would be warm soon.

As the duo entered the station, they saw it was crowded. Jeremy, Mark, and Enzo were there with the other officers.

"Emma!" Jeremy called and walked over to her. He took in her pale face. "Everything all right?"

"It was a bit much," she admitted.

"What was in the eggs?" he asked in a low voice.

"It was a meat puzzle."

"Were all the parts there?"

"We won't know until the coroner finishes his examination."

"We should report to Bill. Where did Jake disappear to?" he asked, looking around.

"His lab, he wants to develop the pictures. I told him we'd wait for him and go home together."

Jeremy rubbed his neck. "Been a long night."

Emma noticed the boys were slumped on a bench asleep. "We need to get them home."

Jeremy turned away from them and went to the clerk's desk. He spoke in a low voice.

"Yeah, we can do that." He called over to another officer. "Charlie, take these boys home."

Charlie moved over to the sleeping boys. He shook their shoulders and asked, "Ready to go home?"

"The folks are gonna be upset," Enzo said with a yawn. Mark sat up, rubbing his eyes.

Jeremy said, "We had an officer let the families know you'd be at our house tonight."

"Good. I don't think I could take any babies crying tonight," Enzo grumbled. Charlie and the boys headed out.

"I need to see that board again," Emma told Jeremy.

"Let's go." He took her hand, and they walked back to the situation room. They stood in front of the map. She took a pin and added the new location. "What're you thinking?"

"There's something about where these scenes have been found," she murmured.

"What is it?"

"I'm not sure," she admitted, "but I think I know someone who might see what we're missing."

CHAPTER 6

The seventh day of Christmas, at the boarding house that next morning

Emma stirred and began to get out of bed.

"Where're you going?" moaned Jeremy, moving his arm to pin her to the bed.

"Up, there's work to be done."

"But we just got to bed," he moaned, but released her.

When she moved to the side of the bed, he followed her and rubbed her shoulders. "At least we have some time now."

"I hope you're right. Finding the swans and the cow will hopefully stop the next two murders." Jeremy didn't say anything as he continued to rub her shoulder. "What's next?" she asked.

"If six, seven, and eight were last night, then in two nights we have the drummers drumming to work on."

"And where do we start with that?"

He dropped down beside her. "We'll have to figure it out. He can't get away with any more murders."

"We have to stop him," she agreed.

Jeremy's stomach rumbled in hunger. "That's odd. The bell isn't ringing for breakfast," he observed.

"Dora might be trying to keep things quiet so the boys can get some rest." Emma tapped him on the shoulder. "Get dressed."

He walked to the bookcase covering the door to his room. "Don't forget Hen's back today."

"I remember. You know, we still need to wrap the presents."

"Tonight," he suggested. "See you on the other side."

"See you," she said and watched him exit. She pulled herself up and moved to get dressed. *Christmas*, she thought. A plaid skirt and a green shirt for the day. She grinned and pulled out green stockings. She went to the dresser to take out a petticoat. "Going to need a new one," she muttered to herself. A knock distracted her. "Just a minute," she called. She pulled on her boots and moved to open the door.

Jeremy stood there waiting. He offered her his elbow. They started downstairs and saw Dora waiting for them at the bottom. Her finger at her lips warned them with a gesture to the sitting room. They nodded and met her in the foyer.

"Are the boys still asleep?" Emma asked in a low voice, glancing into the sitting room. Both boys were sleeping on the floor with blankets and pillows.

"They haven't stirred. Let's leave them be," Dora whispered. They moved into the dining room; the morning was quiet, but Dora pulled the doors closed.

"Jake still asleep?" asked Emma.

Ethyl brought in a pitcher of milk and said, "He's sleeping in." They nodded. When they had finally gotten home, Amy and Ethyl were already in the kitchen baking.

Emma sat down. Jeremy was already filling his plate. Tim walked in and asked the first question.

"I helped you two out last night, so I think we deserve an explanation other than the one you gave us previously."

Jeremy nodded and tapped Emma on the leg. "You're right. This thing is getting bigger not smaller," she said. Dora frowned but didn't ask any questions; she'd save those for later. Emma looked at Patrick with raised eyebrows.

"He can stay," Tim told her. "He's old enough to understand that the world can be a dangerous place." Patrick had stayed quiet and continued to eat. Dora nodded. She and Tim wanted Patrick to be strong, and overprotecting him wasn't the way to do that.

Emma began. "It started two nights ago."

"Did something happen at the restaurant?" asked Dora.

"The apple," Tim muttered. She hadn't stopped talking about it.

"Yes," Dora said, glaring at him, "the apple."

Emma smiled slightly. "You were right, the apple was a clue. I didn't get to eat that night."

"I did, and it was delicious," Jeremy said.

"Oh, shut up," she said and threw a roll at him.

Tim asked, "What happened?"

Emma continued. "We were having dinner. I'd ordered soup as my main meal."

"Not a meal," Jeremy muttered.

Emma ignored him and continued with the story. "With the soup came something none of us ordered."

"What was it?" Tim asked, fascinated.

Jeremy sang, "Five golden rings."

"Like from the song?" Patrick asked.

"That's right," Emma remarked.

"Well, that doesn't sound so bad," Tim said.

"They were still attached to fingers," Jeremy replied laconically. All motion in the room stopped.

"Oh, yuck." Patrick blanched.

Dora looked sick. "Why is it always murders at Christmas?" she groaned.

"I'm not sure," Emma said. "Heightened emotions maybe? Family dynamics? The joy of the season?"

Patrick asked the next question. "Was this the first or fifth murder?"

Jeremy laughed suddenly. "You're fast kid. You got it exactly right. This was the fifth."

"Well," Emma quantified, "the fifth night, but there's been more murders than just one per night; some have been two or three."

"How did you find out about the other murders?" asked Tim.

"When the police responded to the restaurant, they involved us in the investigation," Emma clarified.

"There's already a special team set up with this. We were shown the board that listed the other murders," Jeremy explained.

Patrick frowned. "If the gold rings were two nights ago, what about last night?"

"Last night," Emma said and looked at the closed doors, "the boys stumbled onto the geese, swans, and a cow."

"We believe they also prevented the next two nights of murders from occurring," Jeremy stated.

"At least, we hope so," Emma clarified.

"Are the boys in any danger?" asked Tim.

"We don't think so, but as witnesses, we'll have them watched," Jeremy conceded. "We do believe this is contained to one area at this time."

Emma tapped the table. "Dora, we need to have sketches of the men the boys saw moving the geese."

She nodded. "I can do that."

"We should probably get going," Jeremy told them, checking his watch.

"Yes, the team will be assembling soon."

Emma and Jeremy finished breakfast quickly and moved to the foyer. They pulled on their coats and walked outside. Jeremy had arranged for a carriage, and it stood waiting. Jeremy gave the driver the address and Emma stopped him.

"I think one more stop before that."

"What're you thinking?" asked Jeremy. She leaned in and told him her plans. "That's what we'll do."

~

At the station

"Why aren't the two boys here? We have questions," Coleman demanded.

"They're the reason we found the scene last night," agreed Davies.

"And stopped the next two nights of murder," Williams added.

"Yeah, that's exactly why we need more information," Coleman said.

"The boys are resting," Emma told the men. "They did see two men who were watching the animals. My sister has worked as a sketch artist and said she'd do the drawings."

"Our sketch artist is out of town, and I'm not sure your sister has been vetted by the department," Coleman argued.

"I think it's an excellent idea," McClaughry said as he entered the room. "I'm assuming you mean Dora?" He looked at Emma, and she nodded. "She's approved," he said briskly.

Davies dropped his pencil in frustration. "Sir!"

"You have a complaint, officer? We need whatever help we can get to solve this case," the chief warned.

Davies looked like he might argue the point, but finally relented. "No, sir, I don't."

"Good. I'm eager to see the sketches," McClaughry said and walked to the door. The coroner walked in and the chief delayed his exit to speak to him. "Goldman, what've you found out?"

"We're missing some parts of the body," he muttered.

"Which ones?"

"The other hand, a leg, the chest."

"Bill," the chief called over. Coleman broke away from his group and joined the two men, and Goldman repeated what he'd told the chief. He turned to the other officers.

"Oscar, James, Nelson, we need to search trash bins around that area for missing body parts."

"Yes, sir," the three said and left the room.

"The rest of you, go on and check with the officers in the area." The men left the room.

"I'll head back now," Goldman said and left.

"I'll come with you," the chief said.

A tall, thin man walked past them and into the room. Davies approached him. "You're not supposed to be here. This is a private meeting."

"Yeah, well, Emma asked me to stop by this morning," he said, briefly moving past the officer.

Davies didn't like that, and he grabbed the tall man's arm. "I said you can't come in here!"

"You might stop that before it turns into a brawl," suggested Jeremy. Emma dragged her eyes from the map and saw her friend Harvey clenching his fist.

She hurried over. "Davies, I invited him as a subject matter expert."

Harvey looked pointedly at the hand still gripping his sleeve.

Coleman called over, "Davies, we need you up here." Davies released the man's arm and walked over to Bill at the front of the room.

"Thanks for coming in, Harvey," Emma told her friend.

Harvey's mouth twisted. "I get the feeling I'm not exactly wanted around here."

"We want you. Can you come up and look at the map with us?"

He walked up to the map. He looked at the pins and his gaze drifted up to another location. She told him what had occurred over the past seven days. "The murders are a distraction."

Coleman and Davies walked over to them. "A distraction for what?" Davies shouted. "Who's this guy?"

"Davies, take it down a notch. I would like to hear what he has to say," said Coleman.

Harvey tapped the map. "This is where the final job will be." Emma and Jeremy walked over. It was the richest part of town. Mansions lined the streets.

"But..." stuttered Davies. "That isn't even the right area."

They ignored him and continued their conversation. "Claire's mentioned invitations to some of these Christmas Eve parties," Emma said. "All of the money and jewels will be concentrated there."

"That might be, but we have many murders we need to concentrate on. Where will they strike next?" Coleman asked, trying to step in and direct the conversation. Emma, Jeremy, and Harvey continued to ignore Davies and Coleman.

Slam!

They turned toward the now-shut door. Coleman and Davies were gone.

"Finally," Harvey said. "What's up with him? Both those guys seem like asses."

"Ignore them, Coleman is the lead. He is just a little intense," Jeremy explained. "He seems to have good instincts, though. He's right that the murders will continue, even if the final job is a buildup to a con."

"Hmm," Harvey murmured noncommittally.

"You know, Claire and Thomas are attending at least two of

the parties and wanted us to attend as well," Emma said to Jeremy.

"So, we're planning on attending a party?"

"I guess so," she said, leaning on the desk. "Why don't we let the officers move forward with the murders and make plans for the final Christmas event?"

Havey sat and looked at the two of them. "Have you thought there might be a mole?"

"One of the officers?" Emma asked incredulously.

"Hmmm. I suppose it's possible," Jeremy admitted. "With this kind of thing, the killers like to see the reactions to their work."

CHAPTER 7

Back at the boarding house

"Come on now, boys. Time to get up," Dora called from the sitting room doorway.

"Maybe we should pour a bucket of water on them," Tim suggested as he walked up beside her.

That woke them up! Enzo yawned broadly and asked, "What time is it?"

"11:30."

"You let us sleep a long time," Mark said, scratching his head.

"You deserved it. We heard what you did last night," Tim replied.

"We didn't do much," Mark countered. "We just found some geese."

"You not only found the animals, but you also located a murderer," Dora corrected them.

"And may have prevented two more deaths," Tim said.

"Murders? Did she say murders?" Enzo asked, stopping what he was doing.

"Yeah, that's what it sounded like." Mark called to Dora, "Can we have breakfast?"

"Eggs and toast?"

"Perfect."

"Come into the kitchen."

"Murders," Enzo repeated and helped Mark up. "I didn't know." They followed them through the dining room.

"No, you just wanted to take care of the animals," said Tim.

"How are the animals involved?" Mark asked.

Dora answered, "A madman is using the twelve days of Christmas to set up murder scenes."

Mark frowned. "That wouldn't be right, would it? The song starts on Christmas."

"Someone got it wrong," suggested Mark. He thought about it. "That would mean we are on night seven?"

"You both found night six, and it looks like you might have prevented nights seven and eight."

"That's a mistake, right?" Enzo asked. "Shouldn't he have waited until Christmas?"

"Not the smartest murderer," Mark replied.

"Just keep it quiet for now, please. Emma and Jeremy are working on this with a special police team," Dora appealed.

"We will," the boys said together.

"Let's get you fed," said Dora. They followed her into the kitchen. Ethyl and Amy were working on lunch.

"Do you need me to make them lunch?" asked Amy.

"No, I'll take care of it," Dora told her. She turned to the boys. "Have a seat." She got them some milk and poured it into glasses.

"Thanks," they each said and watched as she got the eggs and butter and moved to the stove.

"Can I help?" asked Mark.

"You can slice some bread and put it in the oven."

He moved over to the bread box and got out a knife. He cut the bread quickly and Ethyl helped him put it in the stove.

Jake entered the kitchen. "Can I get some of those eggs?" he asked.

"Of course, have a seat." Ethyl moved to get him some milk while he joined the boys at the table. She brushed his hair back off his head. He smiled at her.

"Is anyone eating lunch today?" Amy complained.

"Not to worry, the rest of us will be eating lunch." Dora laughed. She finished preparing the eggs and split them into three plates. "The toast is done," Ethyl said, pulling it out. She carried it to the table with some butter and jam.

The three ate until nothing was left. Mark sat back and rubbed his stomach. "I was hungry."

"Well, if you're full..." Dora started.

"We are," Mark and Enzo admitted.

"Then I have another task for you."

"What's that?" asked Mark.

"Emma sent a note over and asked me to sketch the men you saw last night."

Mark looked at Enzo and shrugged. "Sure, I don't see why not."

"Great. Tim's watching Lottie. Let's move to the sitting room." They followed her and sat down. "There are two?" she asked, retrieving her sketch pad.

"Yeah," volunteered Enzo. Mark nodded.

"Okay then, one at a time."

"Both are about the same height," Mark started, remembering the two men at the wagon.

"Yes, but one was slightly taller with dark shaggy hair and a square jaw," Enzo supplied.

"They're both big guys," Mark added.

"They had to be; they needed to move those heavy crates," Enzo reminded his friend.

"What about the eyes?" Dora prompted.

"Smallish," Enzo replied.

"Yeah, that's right, and heavy frown lines on his forehead."

"How old?"

"Old, thirties, I think," Mark added.

"Humph, *old*," Dora muttered, rolling her eyes. She changed out papers. "The other one?"

"He had acne," Mark said.

"Yeah, lightish hair, heavy jowls, bigger eyes than the other guy," Enzo commented.

She nodded and made the change. "Like that?" she asked and showed them the sketch.

"Yeah, that's close," Enzo acknowledged.

"He was older, more like forties," added Mark.

Dora asked additional questions and added the details. She moved the drawing closer to her and finally turned them around. "How about these?"

Enzo looked at them and then at Mark. "That's them!" he exclaimed.

"It's a close likeness," Mark agreed. "What now?"

"I'll get Tim to take these to the police station and they'll decide how to use them." She started to walk away and turned back, "Don't mention the murders, this is a police investigation."

"Okay." Mark nodded. "I need to get home."

"Me, too," Enzo said.

"You sure?" Mark asked his friend.

"Yeah, the folks will be worried."

They put on their coats and headed outside. "Hey," Enzo looked at Mark, "after we check in with the folks, want to go ask about the animals and see if we can help get them back to the zoo?"

"Sounds like a plan," Mark conceded. The two boys went to

their respective homes and shared the story of the animals. They kept the murders under wraps per Dora's instruction. At the police station, the harsh winter wind slammed into the door into the wall as the duo entered. "Get that door closed!" hollered the clerk.

The boys worked together to get the door closed. They turned toward the clerk. "Hey, it's the boys from last night."

"Yeah. We wanted to check on the animals," Enzo replied.

"Mr. DeVry is with them at the horse stalls. You can go over."

"Great," Enzo said.

The two boys headed to the horse stalls and found Mr. DeVry kneeling next to the geese. "Yes, they're all here, but how am I going to them back without help?"

"We'll help, sir," Enzo told the man.

DeVry turned to them, his trademark cigar hanging out of his mouth. He took it out and asked in a rough voice, "What're you doing here around my animals?"

The officer with Mr. DeVry stood up. "Sir, these boys are the ones who saved your animals. They found them and contacted the police."

DeVry charged over to them and put his cigar back in his mouth to pump each of their hands. "Thank you so much."

"We didn't want them to get hurt," Enzo told the man.

"You said you could help me?" DeVry asked. The weather was deteriorating, and he needed them back to a safe environment.

"Yes, sir," Enzo said. Mark nodded.

"I have crates, but we may have to do several trips," DeVry said, chewing on his cigar.

"Do you have someone at the zoo watching things for you?" Mark wondered.

"I do. There are several employees there feeding the animals. I'll have them guard the animals we bring back."

"The geese should be out of danger," Enzo said. Mark knocked him on the shoulder.

DeVry frowned. "Why do you think that? If they came after them once, wouldn't they try again?"

"You're right, sir. I was just thinking out loud."

"Follow me to the wagon," DeVry directed. They followed him out and saw it was full of crates. The boys removed the first one and carried it inside. "We can put two in at a time," he continued. "We'll see how many animals we can get." They got the geese and the swans into the crates. A sudden moo caused them to look toward the back of the barn.

"What about her?" Mark asked, staring at the cow.

DeVry sighed. "Martha will have to stay here until the weather clears up enough for her to walk back."

Enzo studied the cow. "I have an idea. The police have a wagon. I think I could set up a ramp to get her in."

"That would be a relief, my boy. When can you do this?"

"After we get these animals back to the zoo and come back, I'll clear it with the clerk."

DeVry took the cigar out of his mouth. "You have saved the day again."

They lifted the crates. Mark, Enzo, and the officer carried them to the wagon. There were heavy blankets inside. "Drape these over the boxes; we want to keep them as warm as possible," DeVry directed.

After the animals were covered, Enzo rode up front with DeVry and Mark climbed in the back. The trip didn't take too long, and they soon pulled up to the zoo gate. The large sign above the entrance read Lincoln Park Zoo. DeVry handed Enzo the reins and climbed down to unlock the gate. He pushed the gates open and waved Enzo in.

Enzo moved the wagon slowly through the entrance and into the zoo. DeVry waited for them, closed the gates back, and secured the locks. After he locked the gates, DeVry

NOTEBOOK MYSTERIES ~ THE TWELVE DAYS OF MURDER

climbed back on, took the reins, and guided them through the zoo.

Enzo and Mark looked around at the different exhibits with interest. Mark asked, "What other types of animals do you have here?"

"We have four eagles, eight peacocks, three wolves, a puma, two elk, a bear, a bison…"

"Swans, geese, and a cow," finished Enzo.

"That's right, my boy."

"That's amazing."

"Do you boys need a job?" asked DeVry.

"Don't you have personnel here?" Mark inquired.

"I do, but my night man, Gus, left me in a lurch."

"When was this?"

"The night the animals were taken. He must have left and that was when they were able to get in and steal the animals."

Mark's eyes squinted. That sounded important, and he knew he needed to tell Emma and Jeremy. "Sir, once we unload the animals, we should probably go back and get Martha transported."

"That'll be fine. Come see me when you get her back. I'll introduce you to some of the other animals."

"That would be great," Enzo replied.

They pulled up to an enclosure. "During the winter, we like to keep them in a warm location," DeVry explained. "The ice and snow could kill them. Everyone out, let's get 'em inside."

They carefully moved each of the crates inside and into their pens. The animals were released and seemed content to be back home.

"We'll head back to get things organized for Martha," Enzo said.

DeVry nodded and watched his animals. "You can take the wagon to get you back there."

"Yes, sir. Thank you."

"Jim!" DeVry called.

"Yes, you wanted me?" An older man walked up. He was dressed in rough work clothes and was rubbing his hand on a towel.

"Make sure the gate is locked behind them."

He nodded and called to the boys, "When you're ready."

"Now would be good," Mark replied. They headed back out to the wagon. Enzo and Mark sat up front, and Jim in back. At the gate, Jim jumped out and opened it for them.

"Jim," called Mark, "what did Gus, the man who worked nights, look like?"

"Blond shaggy hair, light build, kind of lanky."

"Thanks," Mark said as Enzo started to guide the wagon through the gate.

Jim stopped them with a hand held up. "It's odd, you know..."

"What's that?"

"He loved his job. He didn't make much, but the animals made him happy."

"He hadn't done this before?"

"Leave without notice?" They nodded. "No." Jim backed up and let them go on their way. They waved at him as they drove out the gate.

Enzo asked in a low voice, "What was that about?"

"I think I know where Gus is."

"How would you know that?"

"Trust me, I know." Mark had seen the head before Emma covered it last night. "What're we doing here?" he asked his friend as they pulled up to a dilapidated house.

"Getting wood for the ramp so we can move Martha," Enzo explained.

"You're assuming they won't mind if you borrow the big wagon."

"Yeah, I think I can convince them."

"Right," Mark replied, his mind on Gus.

They went inside the house and found Michael, Enzo's dad.

"Hey, Dad."

"Enzo, you working with me today?"

"No, sir, I'm helping out with Mr. DeVry from the zoo."

He nodded. "Then what're you doing here?"

"We need some wood for a ramp. There's a cow that needs to get back to her home at the zoo."

"We wouldn't want to walk her there," Mark commented.

"Not in this weather," Michael agreed.

They all picked up the wood to build a ramp and tools to pile in the wagon. *Emma and Jeremy should be at the station*, Mark thought. When they arrived at the barn, Enzo parked the wagon outside and unhitched the horse. "I don't want her to get too cold before we return her."

"Good idea," Mark replied. "Let's hit the station next to make sure we can use the big wagon." Mark and Enzo went into the station and were able to confirm quickly that the wagon was available to transport Martha.

"Do you need some help with that ramp?" asked the clerk.

"We could use the help," Enzo admitted.

He called to several officers behind them. "Go help these boys build a ramp." The officers followed the boys out to the barn. The ramp came together quickly, and Martha was slowly moved outside and into the wagon. Once the doors were closed, Mark turned to Enzo. "I need to get with Emma on something."

"Go on. We'll get Martha and the wagons back."

"Thanks!"

Enzo and the officers piled into the wagons for the trip back to the zoo. They needed to get the Zoo wagon back as well as the wagon with Martha. Mark ran up the stoop into the precinct and the clerk looked up. "Back again? Animals all gone?"

"Yeah. We just got the cow loaded into the wagon. The officers will drop off the cow and come back."

"Good, I hate to see any animals mistreated."

"Me, too." He looked around and asked, "Are Emma and Jeremy here?"

"I think they're in the situation room."

"Can I go back?"

"Sure, you know the way?"

"I do."

The clerk went back to his paperwork and Mark went down a long hallway. He looked into each room and found Emma, Jeremy, and Cole in the last one. He knocked lightly on the door; they seemed to be in an intense conversation.

Emma looked over in surprise. "Mark, what're you doing here?"

"Me and Enzo wanted to help move the animals back to the zoo."

"Oh, that's nice of you."

"Are they all settled?" asked Jeremy.

"Yeah, thank goodness. We took the geese and swans earlier, and Enzo just left with the cow."

Cole said, "We might still want guards on the swans and the cow for the next two nights. I'll send some men over there."

"That's what I wanted to talk with you about," Mark said, twisting his hands.

"What is it, Mark?" asked Emma as she walked over to him.

"I think I might know who was in the eggs last night."

Emma frowned. "I didn't realize you saw anything."

"I did, right before you covered it up," he confirmed.

Jeremy asked, "Who do you think it is?"

"There's a man missing from the night shift at the zoo. He took care of the animals at night," he explained.

"Mr. DeVry didn't mention it," Cole said.

"He thought he just quit his job and disappeared."

"But you don't?"

"The timing seems odd," Mark admitted.

"He's got good instincts," Emma said, looking at Cole and Jeremy. "Do you know what the man looked like?"

"Blond shaggy hair, lean guy."

Jeremy looked at Emma. She nodded. "It fits."

"We'll need someone to identify him," Cole said.

"Mr. DeVry," Emma and Mark said together. She laughed and roughed up his hair.

∾

Mr. DeVry at the coroner's office

"I guess I have to be here?" DeVry asked gruffly.

"I understand there's no one else. He wasn't married?" Coleman asked. He'd been briefed about the identification and had DeVry transported over. Emma and Jeremy had accompanied them.

"No, I can do it. I feel bad that I thought he ran off; he loved the animals. I should've known better." They didn't say anything, they just let him talk.

"This will be graphic. Can you manage it?" the coroner asked.

DeVry swallowed and nodded. The coroner lowered the sheet, and the blond hair was visible. DeVry nodded slowly, his Adam's apple going up and down, his face turning green. He croaked, "It's him." DeVry started to gag.

"Get him out of here. I don't want to clean that up!" The coroner ordered.

Emma and Jeremy grabbed DeVry and ran him out into the snow. He leaned over and took several deep breaths.

"Are you going to be sick?" Emma asked, concerned.

He took some snow and plopped it on his neck. "No, I'll be

okay. Gus won't be, though. Who'd want to hurt a man who only thought was to help animals?"

"I don't know, sir. I just don't know," Emma said.

~

Boarding house, Tim and Dora

Tim walked over to Dora with Lottie. "How did they turn out?" She laid the drawings down and took Lottie from him. Tim picked them up and examined them. "The boys said they were pretty accurate," she said.

"Do you want me to run them over to the station?"

"Yes, please," she said at the same moment the door swung open.

Hen yelled behind her, "Bye!"

"Henrietta," Dora called, "did you have a good time?"

The girl ran over to Dora for a hug. Lottie giggled. "I did. Are Jeremy and Emma home?"

Dora brushed the snow off Hen's coat. "No, they're out for a while. You want to hang out with me and Lottie?"

Before she could answer, Henrietta saw Tim. "Hey, Tim."

"Hey, Hen."

"What do you have there?" she asked.

"Sketches," he said, keeping them turned toward him.

"You can show her," Dora told him.

Tim handed the sketches to the girl. "Who are they?" she asked, examining them.

"They're bad guys, and if you ever see them, report it immediately."

"Is this part of the new case?" Hen asked.

"It is, and I'll tell you about it later, but for now Tim needs to go out."

At that moment, Patrick ran in. "Can I go with you, Papa?"

"Sure, grab your hat and coat."

"You boys have a nice time. Be careful," Dora told them.

Tim kissed Dora's cheek. "We might do a little Christmas shopping," said Tim.

"Well, then take your time." Dora chuckled.

Patrick mumbled through his muffler, "Bye!"

Tim and Patrick made their way by carriage to the station. He paid the driver and asked, "Can you wait? We need to do some shopping."

"I'll wait. Not too long, though," he cautioned. "The wind's started to pick up."

"We'll be quick," Tim promised. He and Patrick went into the station. "Is Emma or Jeremy around?" he asked the clerk.

"They're in the situation room. Officer, take these two back."

"Yes, sir, follow me."

Tim followed the officer down the hallway. The door was open, and they could see Jeremy and Emma at a board. Jeremy spotted him and nudged Emma. She nodded and continued to talk to a man in front of them. Jeremy walked over to Tim.

"Are those the sketches?"

"It is. The boys said they're accurate."

"Great. I'll make sure we get copies and distribute them." Tim and Patrick started to head out. "Hold it, where're you headed?"

"Christmas shopping."

Jeremy bent down and said, "Avoid the Liberty Park area. We think he's using that area to pick his victims."

"Got it." Tim and Patrick headed out.

Jeremy walked up to the clerk. "Do you have the mimeograph copier Ellis donated?"

"Sure, what do you need copied?"

"These two sketches."

"I'll take care of it." The copies were made and passed out to all of the officers going into the situation room. One of the officers stood in the hallway with his copy. "Shit," he said, crinkling the paper up into a small ball. This was exactly what he didn't need.

Coleman stood in front of Emma and said, "We still have two days before the ninth day of Christmas." He turned to the group. "Everyone come in and get settled." They moved to their seats and the room quieted. "We've called you back to get the sketches and to get ideas from you on what the drummer's drumming could be."

"Bands!" called out one of the officers.

"Professional and school kids," Williams said.

Jeremy flipped through the paper and laid it down in front of Emma. She raised an eyebrow at him, and he tapped on the paper. She looked down. "A parade," she whispered.

"Yeah. Where else would you find the required drummers drumming?" he replied in a low voice.

The group was still talking about where they could find bands. "How about the parade?" Emma spoke up. "It works for the drummers and is the right night."

Both Coleman and Davies frowned at the interruption. One of the officers spoke up. "Hey, there's going to be a parade. It's a few days from now."

"That's good work, Peters! A parade," Coleman said. "We'll need to work in groups."

"Didn't I just say a parade?" Emma asked Jeremy.

"I heard you say a parade," he replied.

Willians spoke up. "Sir, there're fifteen bands and innumerable drummers. We don't have the resources to cover that."

"We could cancel the parade," suggested Davies.

Everyone looked at him incredulously and Coleman finally said, "You've to be kidding. The mayor would have a nervous breakdown."

"So, what do we do?"

"We assign several officers to each band and inspect the drums before they get started."

The men were dispatched, and Emma and Jeremy were left alone. "Coulda sworn I said a parade," she muttered and looked at Jeremy. "Well, I guess that leaves us."

"It's different when it isn't our case. We should update Pops."

"We can look ahead into the parties, per Harvey's suggestion. That'll probably be up to us. These guys aren't focused past the next event."

"Then we'll do that."

"We should head to Claire's office. She has the information on the parties."

"Sounds like a plan."

"I know I said a parade," Emma said as they were leaving.

"I know you did, babe," Jeremy said in commiseration.

Carriages were getting harder to come by the worse the weather got. "The parade will be a cold event this year," Emma observed.

"Yeah, but people will still show up." They walked a few blocks, huddled together. "Finally," he said and waved his arm to a carriage. It pulled up and Jeremy called out the address.

They climbed in and a familiar voice said, "I was on my way to see you both."

"Cole!"

"This works out perfectly," Jeremy told him. "We were on our way to catch you up, Pops."

"Tell me." They went over the morning meeting. "Harvey has the right idea about the misdirection," Cole agreed, stroking his goatee. "We will manage the party. I'll get with Chief McClaughry about using Pinkerton's undercover at the parties. Where're you headed now?"

"Claire's office to go over the list of parties to see which ones might be targets," Emma said.

"These the same ones you normally avoid?" teased Cole.

"Well, if you remember the party we had last year at Geoff and Gregory's, all the others seem to pale in comparison," she teased back.

"Ah, yeah. Good ole Geoff and Gregory. Good times," Jeremy said.

Cole dropped them at Claire's office. "I'll come by this evening to confirm the plans."

They ran into the building and shook off the snow as they entered. They waved at the guard; he knew them by sight and waved back.

The elevator door opened, and the operator leaned out. "Miss Evans, Mr. Tilden, fourth floor?"

"Yes, please," Jeremy said.

They rode up, silently watching the number increase. "Thank you, Charlton," Emma said as they stepped into the long hall and approached the double doors to the foundation's office. Jeremy pushed them open, and they went in.

"Emma! Jeremy!" Hen called as she ran over to them.

"Hen! What're you doing here?" Jeremy asked, giving her a quick hug.

"Tim brought me over when he needed to drop some things off with Nathan."

"Is he still here?"

"He's downstairs," she confirmed. "I just wanted to come visit."

Claire walked over to hand her secretary, Lily, a stack of papers. "Finally," Claire said, "we have to go over these invitations."

"Yes, we do," Emma said.

Claire frowned. "I'm sorry. I don't think I heard you correctly. Did you say you want to go over the invitations?"

"As cofounders of this foundation, I think it's time we stepped up and started attending these parties."

"Uh huh," Claire said dubiously. "As long as I've known you

two, you've been putting off going to parties. You don't know how many potential investors have begged to see the 'famous girl detective' and you've flat out ignored them."

"She's got you there, babe." Jeremy snickered.

"You want to tell me what's really going on?" Claire asked.

"Well…" Emma stammered. "Alright, fine. We have reason to believe—reasons that we can't go into right now—that one of these parties will be the scene of a crime. We need to look for the most obvious ones so we can prevent it."

"Now, that wasn't so hard, was it? Would you like to look through the invitations now?"

"I do. And we'll need to look at a map. Hen, can you hang out here with Lily?" Emma asked the girl.

"Does this have anything to do with those bad people that Dora was sketching today?"

"You know about that, huh?" Emma asked.

"Tim showed me the sketches. Dora said it was okay."

"Dora was right," Emma said.

"Soooo… can I come in and hear what's happening?"

Claire waited for their decision.

Emma finally said, "You're old enough to understand, but don't share anything you might hear. Okay?"

"Okay."

They walked into the office and Jeremy pulled the doors closed behind them. Claire walked to her desk and pulled out the invitations. She plopped the pile down onto the desk in front of her. "Do you want to explain why I need a map to review these with you?"

Emma gave her a quick rundown of the last few days. "So, Harvey thinks this whole thing is leading to a larger scam, a money grab."

"So many people will die getting to the last night," Claire lamented.

"Mark and Enzo stopped many more murders."

"They also gave us a few days to breathe," Jeremy said.

"You hope," Claire replied.

Jeremy bent down in front of Hen. "Do you have any questions?"

"Dora and Tim explained the case to me," she said.

"And you'll come to us if you have any other questions?"

"I will." She hugged him.

Claire pulled out the map and they used a pen to mark the locations of the parties.

"Another grouping," commented Emma.

"Yeah, but it's farther away from the area where the bodies are turning up," Jeremy said.

"So, we know it's probably this area," said Claire, circling an area, "but which one?"

"Can you give us an idea of who's giving each party?" Emma asked her friend.

"Let's move to the table." They followed her and sat at her round table. Claire opened each invitation, discussing the family or business that would be at each party. They'd gone through more than ten and Emma slumped back in her chair. "So many," she said wearily. "We need a way to narrow this down."

Jeremy had picked up the unopened envelopes and flipped through them. He stopped and held up one up. "I'll bet it's this one."

"Why that one?" Emma asked. He didn't answer; he just handed her the envelope.

She took it and examined who it was from. "You know what? I think that will do it," she confirmed.

"What am I missing?" Claire asked, looking at both of them.

Emma read out loud, "Lord Cedrick Brunsby is in town and will be receiving guests at the Nickerson estate for Christmas."

"Lords a-leaping!" shouted Hen.

"Sounds like the most likely scenario," Jeremy confirmed.

"Then we go to that one," Claire said. "I'll also need to attend at least four others that evening."

"I like that. RSVP for all of the ones you think we should attend," Emma told her.

"Why do that when you only need the one?" Hen asked curiously.

"Harvey thinks, and we agree, that there's a mole in the police dept. Someone either directly involved in the case or supplying information to the murderer."

Claire looked at Hen. "I think I hear Thomas out in the office. Can you get him for me?"

"I'll get him," she said, running to the door.

"I love it when she's here. She keeps us on our toes," Claire confessed.

"She does that at home also," admitted Emma.

"Emma!" Hen called and ran to her. "Thomas says there's a Christmas parade! Can we go? I want to go."

Emma looked at Jeremy, and he shrugged. "Can we talk about it at home?" she asked Hen.

"If you can't take her, she is welcome to go with us," Claire spoke up.

"It should be fun," said Thomas.

"Let's think about it," Jeremy requested. "Drummers drumming," he said to Emma.

"Drummers drumming?" Claire asked. "Should we not go?"

"What's this about drums?" asked Thomas.

"Murder!" Hen told him.

"Murder?" he asked faintly.

"I'll explain later," Claire told her husband.

"Can we go now?" Hen asked Emma and Jeremy.

Jeremy looked at her. "Get your coat and hat, then we can go." She ran to get her coat.

"We should stop on the way out and see if Tim wants to join us," suggested Emma.

"I'm ready," called Hen, her hat and coat on her arm.

Jeremy held out his elbow to each of them. They each took a side and Emma called out, "Have a nice evening."

Lily, Thomas, and Claire watched them leave.

"What was that about?" Lily asked. "I thought we were going to have to force them to go to any parties."

"A lot's going on. Lily, you need to come hear about this also," Claire said and walked with Thomas to her office. Lily laid down her papers and followed them.

～

Hen continued to chatter about the parade. "I can't wait. You don't have to work, do you? Thomas and Claire said I could go with them if you're busy."

Jeremy pushed the button to call the elevator. "Hen, are you okay with the information that was shared with you today?" he asked.

"Yes."

"Will it give you nightmares?" Emma asked. Hen had finally settled in and had put the nightmares behind her.

"I'm fine. I know that you and Jeremy will protect me," the girl said confidently.

The elevator doors opened, and they went in. "Nathan's office, please," Emma told the operator.

"Coming up," Charlton answered as he turned the lever and the car began to move. They looked at the numbers move and the doors opened. At the end of the long hallway, there was a familiar set of double doors. When they pushed open these doors, the area that opened in front of them was very different from that of the foundation. There were desks lined up from one end to the other, with a man at each one working diligently.

The side office door opened, and a smiling Tim exited with

Nathan Lombard, their accountant. They walked over to greet them. "How did you know we were here?" Tim asked.

"We happened to be in the building," Emma replied. "Hi, Nathan."

"Emma, Jeremy, and, Hen, it's always good to see you."

"It was a surprise!" Hen said. "Tim, did you know there's a parade?"

"I heard that, in just a few days."

"We have a carriage waiting," Jeremy said, "if you'd like a ride home."

"I would." He turned to Nathan. "I'll see you after the holidays for the year-end statements."

"I look forward to it," commented Nathan.

"Time to go," said Jeremy.

"Merry Christmas, Nathan!" Hen called.

"Merry Christmas to you all," Nathan replied.

"Don't forget to bring Lily for Christmas dinner," Emma reminded him.

"We're planning on it," Nathan said cheerfully.

∿

Dinner that night

Dora sat with Emma at the dining room table. The kids had moved to the sitting room and were playing games with Jeremy and Tim. "Will there or won't there be a murder tonight?" Dora asked.

"That's the question. I hope not," Emma admitted. "Finding the geese, swans, and cow should stop the next few murders. The police are in charge of it, and they're not taking our advice."

"What will you do?"

"We'll continue to work on days nine through twelve."

"Emma, is it safe to go to the parade? The kids are looking forward to it," Dora fretted.

"The police will be surrounding the different bands."

"The drummers will be their focus, though."

"They will, and we'll all be together."

Dora stood suddenly and took a deep breath. "Murder at this time of year." She looked at the decorations and the nativity. "It just isn't right."

Emma linked arms with her, and they moved into the room with the family. The tree was brightly lit, presents piled under it. Jeremy, Tim, and Patrick were involved in a lively card game on the floor. Lottie and Hen were playing with their dolls.

"Anyone want some treats?" asked Amy as she carried in a tray of cookies. Cole followed her with two pitchers, one for the adults and one for the kids.

Hen went over to take a cookie and held up a glass to the pitcher. "Eggnog, please." Cole poured her a glass. "What's in the other one?" she asked.

"Ah ah, it's for adults only. Mulled wine."

Emma went over to get a whiff of the pitcher. "Hmmm, you can smell the cinnamon, cloves, and nutmeg."

"And the brandy," Jeremy said. "Pour me some, please. Make it a double." The evening stayed quiet, with Emma sending furtive glances at her watch. "We may have made it without anyone getting hurt," he murmured.

"You don't think that the police would hide anything from us, do you?"

"No, it's too big and the chief would force Bill to get in touch with us. You know, we need to stay up late to wrap presents," he murmured. "Hen's been checking for her name under the tree."

"Dora's put several for her."

"Yeah, but she's looking for ones from us."

"I know. We'll make sure they're there when she looks in the morning. I'm looking forward to that being the reason we're up late," she said, laying her head on his shoulder.

CHAPTER 8

The eighth day of Christmas, the next morning

Jeremy and Emma woke surrounded by wrapped presents. "Did we go overboard a little this year?" she asked.

"No, it's best to spoil family at Christmas."

"Why don't we plan a trip to the beach after all of this is finished?" she suggested.

"Just us?"

"No, I was thinking of the whole family."

"It'll be crowded," he said.

"It'll be wonderful. I love the beach in winter."

"All right, get up. We've got things to do, people to see, money to spend," Jeremy needled.

"Aw, just a few more minutes." Emma snuggled closer to him.

"All right, you talked me into it."

"No knocks on the door last night," Emma said after a few minutes.

"Nope. I hope it meant nothing happened."

"Me, too." They lay there quietly. "What's the plan today?" Emma asked.

"Well, if no swans or bodies show up, then we hope it's the same on the ninth night."

"The parade's tomorrow; the whole family will be there."

"They'll be safe. The attacks, if any, are targeted at the drummers. It'll be good for us to be extra eyes and maybe prevent anyone else from getting hurt."

"Sounds like a plan." She sat up.

Jeremy grabbed her and pulled her on top of him. "You know, we can take a minute more."

"Oh, we can, can we?" she asked and lowered her head to his. It was a little while before they were downstairs for breakfast.

"You're late for breakfast this morning," Hen scolded them.

"Couldn't be helped," Emma replied, taking a bite of a biscuit.

"Why not?" the girl pressed.

"Yeah, why not?" Jeremy teased in a low voice.

Emma answered loudly, "Because someone was wrapping presents for someone in this room."

"Many someone's in this room," Jeremy remarked.

Dora lifted Lottie from her chair. "What did you get me?" she asked sweetly.

"I'm not telling; you have to wait for Christmas."

"Hmm."

Tim and Patrick walked in from the kitchen. "What're you and Jeremy up to today?" he asked Emma.

"We have some ideas about going to the station around ten or eleven. They may not want us there, but we're going anyway."

Emma and Jeremy finished eating and carried their plates into the kitchen. Ethyl and Amy were there finishing the dishes. "Sorry we held you up," Emma told the two women.

"That's fine, a few more won't hurt," Amy replied.

"Do you need me to pick up some Christmas cookies or cakes for tonight?" she asked.

"That'd be nice. Everyone's coming over tonight." Emma walked over to Amy and whispered, "And Cole, too?"

Amy turned red. "None of that. Off with you both."

Emma turned to Jeremy. "You want to help me move the Christmas presents downstairs?"

"After you." He accompanied her up the stairs. "What did you say to rattle Amy?"

"Oh, nothing. I just teased her."

"I'll have to follow up on that later."

"Where're you going?" yelled Hen.

Emma smiled and continued up. Jeremy turned to the girl and said, "Wait for us in the sitting room and you'll see." He grinned as he watched her run into the sitting room. He turned back and went to Emma's room. He opened the door and could see Emma gathering presents.

"She's waiting..." he said.

"Well, don't just stand there. Start picking up the gifts," she said dryly. He followed her lead and picked up as many packages as he could carry.

"I'm *waiting*," Hen called.

Emma smiled. "You know, I kinda like this parenting thing."

"It's not bad at all," he agreed.

They started downstairs and saw Hen in the foyer. She raced back into the sitting room. "So patient," Emma murmured and entered the room. "Were you waiting for us right there?" she teased.

"I haven't moved a muscle," she said. "Are any of those for me?"

"Maybe. Why don't you come over and help us lay them under the tree."

"Can I?"

"Come on," Jeremy said, handing her some of the boxes. She moved them to the tree and carefully placed them underneath.

"We have more over here," Emma said.

"Do we have to wait for Christmas?" asked Hen, gazing longingly at the gifts.

"We do," Jeremy told her.

"Hen, we have many fun activities between now and then, and it'll be here before you know it."

"That's right, the parade's tomorrow."

Jeremy checked his watch. "Babe, we should make an appearance at the police station."

"Wanna get our coats?" she asked.

"Sure, I'll get them."

"Can I go with you?" asked Hen.

"No, I don't think so," he said from the doorway. He held up Emma's coat and she walked over to get it.

Emma murmured into his ear, "Why not take her? Papa took us everywhere with him."

"And look how you turned out," he retorted. He turned back to Hen. She sat on the couch, kicking the leg of the table. "Hen." When she didn't look up, he said her name again. "Hen."

"Yeah?" she mumbled, still not looking up at them.

Emma walked over to the closet and got her coat. "Hen, time to go."

"Really?" She jumped up and ran over to hug first Jeremy, then Emma.

"It's cold, put on your coat." She did and Jeremy pulled her hat over her ears.

"All set?"

"Wait!" called Dora. "Is Hen going with you?"

"She is."

"Don't forget we have the family here tonight."

"We'll be here," Jeremy promised and walked outside to hail a carriage. He waved toward Emma and Hen and they left the house, carefully making their way down the stoop. Jeremy assisted them into the carriage. Once inside, they huddled together.

"What're you doing at the station?" asked Hen.

"We want to get an update on tonight," said Emma.

"And make some progress on Piper's piping," said Jeremy.

"Do we, though?" she wondered out loud.

"What do you mean?" he asked.

"If there's a mole, we tell them exactly what we think is next."

"That's something to think about."

~

At the police precinct, the clerk called, "Pinkertons are getting smaller."

"I'm not a Pinkerton," said Hen.

The clerk said, "You can go back to the situation room." He looked at Hen and asked, "Would you like to stay here and assist me?"

"Can I?" asked Hen.

Jeremy nodded and said a silent "Thanks" to the clerk.

"I have lots for you to help with."

They went to the situation room and took a seat. Emma and Jeremy looked around the room. "Any guesses on who it is?" he asked.

"No, especially in their blues, they all look like heroes, not bad guys."

"We just have to watch and see who tries to pull us off the path."

Coleman walked into the back of the room. "Back again?"

"The chief requested it, Bill," Jeremy said with a long stare.

Coleman nodded and said, "I need to start the meeting." He strode to the front of the room.

"He's on the list, for sure," said Emma.

"He certainly doesn't seem to want your help," an officer said from behind them. They turned to see the young redheaded officer. His freckles stood out on his white face. "Hey, I'm Fred Smith."

"Nice to meet you, Fred," Emma greeted. Jeremy held out his hand to the man. Fred took it and shook it warmly.

"You, too."

"You weren't with us yesterday," commented Emma.

"I was here, but didn't join this group until this morning. I traveled down from upper New York. They asked for extra help with the parade." Emma and Jeremy looked around; there were a lot of new faces in the room.

Coleman started the meeting. "Quiet down, we have an update. Williams, you're up."

The officer stood and went to the front of the room. "It looks like the two boys thwarted last night's murders."

"Nothing was found last night?" called one of the officers.

"No, and we believe this murderer wants attention. So, it would've been found before midnight last night," Williams said.

"The officers at the zoo confirmed that the swans weren't disturbed again," Coleman continued. "Tonight, we're going out on the same rounds as we did last night. This time, it's cows."

"Those might be easier to get somewhere else. Why take them from the zoo?" Peters asked.

"Probably, she was in the right place and, when they took the swans, they took her also," Williams said.

Coleman took over from there. "We'll maintain the rounds, but we need to concentrate on the parade. We've made all the preparations; two teams will work with each band. I have a list here that we'll distribute to each of you." He took the stack of papers from the desk and started circulating them around the room. "Any questions?"

"Seems they have everything under control," Jeremy said to Emma.

"No mention of the pipers," she muttered. "They're not thinking ahead." They watched the men pile out of the room. They stayed where they were.

Coleman shook his head. "You still here?"

"We wanted to talk about the piper's piping," Emma began.

"Look, I have my hands full with the next few nights…" He looked over their shoulders, his spine stiffened, and his jaw tightened. They turned to the door to see what caused the change in the man's demeanor. Chief McClaughry stood at the door with Cole.

"I believe you were discarding advice. Do go on," McClaughry said.

"Sir, I just have my hands full with the next two nights. The parade…"

"So, you're admitting you need help?"

"No, sir, I wasn't saying that. Not exactly."

"Then sit down and let's discuss the pipers."

Coleman sighed and turned the chairs in front of Emma and Jeremy. He waited until Cole and the chief sat down. He took a seat and asked, "What exactly is a piper?"

"Bagpipes," said the chief.

"How are we supposed to find every piper in Chicago?"

McClaughry raised his eyebrow. "Francis O'Neill."

"Does he know someone?"

"He's not only a good policeman," McClaughry said, "but also a talented musician. He plays the flute and Uilleann pipes, sometimes known as Irish pipes. He also associates with a local group of musicians in the immigrant Irish community."

"Where can we find him?" asked Cole.

"He's on shift," Coleman muttered.

"Bill, why don't you see if he has time to consult with us?" the chief suggested.

Coleman stood, knocking his chair over, and stormed out of the room. Cole looked over at the chief and asked, "Is he the right leader for this task force?"

McClaughry rubbed his chin. "It's hard for him to ask for help. I think this'll force him to acknowledge that sometimes it's necessary."

Emma understood that, as she'd had this problem in the past.

Coleman and another man walked back into the room. The other man was a handsome man with pleasant features, a bushy mustache, and chestnut hair.

"You asked for me, sir?"

"I did. Frank, this is Cole Tilden, his son Jeremy, and Emma Evans. They're with the Pinkertons."

"Nice to meet you," Frank said and waited.

"Bill, why don't you go over what we currently have and how Frank can help us?" McClaughry asked.

"Frank, are you up to date on the events?"

"The twelve days of Christmas murders?"

"Yeah. We're on day eight."

"Piper's piping is day ten," Frank supplied. The group nodded in response.

"Are there any events occurring in three days' time?" Emma asked him.

Frank sat back and said, "Yes, John Ennis is in town for a large piping event. All of the most talented pipers in the area will be there."

"Then I assume you'll be there?" the chief asked.

"Well, I do like to pipe," Frank admitted.

"How well do you know Ennis?"

"I know him very well. He's a good man. I've been trying to get him on the force for several years."

"Frank's building a police force that can also play concerts," the chief teased.

Frank turned red. "They're all good men."

"They are indeed," the chief agreed.

"Do you think Ennis would meet with us?" Jeremy asked.

Frank looked at Coleman and the chief. "If you're okay with me taking them over, we can meet with Ennis and discuss the event."

McClaughry looked at Coleman with narrowed eyes. Coleman responded, "Yeah, that'd be good. Report back to me."

"Yes, sir," Frank replied.

The chief stood. "Frank, walk me to the door." Frank followed him to the door.

"Emma and Jeremy, wait for me," Cole said. He joined the two men at the door and shook their hands.

Bill looked at the trio standing at the door and turned back to Emma and Jeremy. He leaned into them. "This is my task force," he said menacingly, "so if you think you're going to waltz in here and grab all of the glory, you're mistaken."

"Bill," Jeremy said, leaning toward him, "if you're in this for the glory, then I think you should switch jobs. This is about the people."

"Now, see here, you little punk," Coleman stormed, his voice heated.

"Bill!" McClaughry warned.

"This ain't settled, not by a long shot," Coleman snarled before he stood and walked up to the door.

Emma's mouth twisted into a semblance of a smile. "What a jackass."

"Yeah, he's going to get the help if he wants it or not," Jeremy agreed.

Cole walked back into the room. "That Bill is some piece of work."

"Yeah, he is."

Frank walked back to them and pulled up a chair. "We're talking the pipers?"

"We are," Cole said. "Tell us about Ennis."

"I have his address. He's currently in Chicago for the event. He's spent the last few years in Nebraska."

"What kind of event will this be?" asked Emma. "What size crowd should we expect?"

"It'll be held in a large assembly room."

"Is it more contained?"

"In comparison to the parades, it'd appear that way. For this type of event, it'll be well attended."

"Who'll be there?" asked Cole.

"All of the pipers in the area will be there, as well as their families."

"So, we'll have at least nine pipers in one location?"

"There'll be at least that number there, if not more," Frank confirmed. "When would you like to go see Ennis?"

"As soon as possible."

Frank stood and said, "I'll need to let my captain know of our plans. Should I meet you back here?"

"Yes, please, and thank you for the help," said Cole.

Jeremy stood. "I'll walk you to the door." Frank departed and Jeremy pulled the door shut.

"What's up?" Cole asked.

Emma started. "We think that there might be a mole on the task force."

"What's your evidence?" he asked.

"We're not sure," Jeremy admitted. "Right now, it's just a gut feeling."

"We also think there is misdirection for ideas on the next steps," Emma continued.

"That could just be Bill wanting to be in charge of everything," Cole suggested.

"It could," she admitted.

"We should focus on our plans and have Pinkerton detectives fill in the gaps," Cole said.

"But the twelfth night is ours," said Emma.

"Yes, we'll be handling that. I've called many men in to work as servers."

"Christmas Eve, big ask."

"All have been volunteers; no one likes the idea of Christmas being used for murder."

A knock sounded on the door and Frank stuck his head in. "If you're ready, we can go over to Ennis' place and discuss the event."

Cole checked his watch. "We can go over there now," he said.

"We need to get Hen," said Jeremy.

"I saw her in the front office. We can pick her up on the way out." Hen joined them and they gathered their things and went out into the cold to their carriage. Once in the carriage, Emma asked, "How are we going approach this?"

"I find honesty is the best policy," said Frank.

"I agree," Cole said.

"And if he wants to cancel?" Jeremy asked.

"Then we'll have to convince him to go through with it and protect them and their families," Emma replied.

"I don't think he'll cancel," Frank told them. "These events take a lot of planning."

"We'll see," Emma said.

They stopped in front of a modest home. It was well taken care of, and the snow was cleared from the walk up to the house. "Are we ready?" asked Cole. Jeremy, Emma, and Frank nodded. Jeremy stepped out and helped Emma down. The wind caught her skirt and pushed it up. She struggled to keep it down and he grabbed the back of it and yelled over the wind, "We need to get inside!"

Cole yelled up to the driver, "We'll check to see if they're home. If they are, come back in an hour for us."

The driver waved to them. They walked quickly up the steps. Cole knocked loudly on the door. When no one answered, he banged on the door again. The door opened and revealed a tallish man in his thirties. He had a grayish mustache and beard. He was a solemn-looking man. The wind blew the door into him, and he spoke with an Irish accent. "You might as well come in." Cole waved to the driver, and he pulled away. They followed his direction and entered.

"Mr. Ennis," Cole started.

Ennis grinned suddenly. "Francis, I don't know how I missed you there. Welcome. It's grand to see you, boyo."

Frank stepped up to Ennis and they shook hands. "I haven't had a chance to come by. It's good to see you."

"I hope you join us for our event."

"John, that's why we're here." Frank's tone turned serious.

"And who might we be?" Ennis asked looking over the group.

Cole stepped up. "I'm Cole Tilden of the Pinkerton Detective Agency; this is Emma Evans and my son Jeremy."

"And me," said Hen.

Emma laid her hands on her shoulders and said, "This is Hen, our daughter."

Hen grinned brightly at the description.

"Papa," called a young child's voice. Three boys ran out of the back of the house; the two older boys pulled a baby with them.

"Boys, hold up, we have guests. Why don't you go back to the kitchen with Mama?"

"Papa, we want to stay with you!" the two boys began yelling.

"Mama!" John called over their yelling.

"Yes?" she asked and saw they had guests. "Welcome. I'll take the boys with me." She started to pull them away.

"Oh, Ma! We want to stay!"

"Come on now, I have cookies. Would you like some?" she asked.

"Yes, please," the two older boys yelled, and the baby grinned.

"I would like some cookies," said Hen.

"Then come with me," she directed all the children. They followed close behind her.

Once the room quieted down, Ennis turned to the trio and waved to the sitting room on his left. "Come in here where it's warmer." The roaring fire drew them in. Emma and Jeremy took the couch, and the men sat across from them in chairs. "Now, what makes you all get out in this weather?" he asked.

Cole spoke first. "Sir, we wanted to talk with you about some events that have been occurring in the area."

"The murders," Ennis said.

"What've you heard, John?" Frank asked.

"Just that people are being targeted," he admitted.

Jeremy asked, "Have you been told how they're linked?"

"No, I can't say I have."

"John, there's a connection to a Christmas song," Frank said.

Ennis frowned at that and waited.

"The Twelve Days of Christmas," Emma explained.

"Or the Twelve Murders of Christmas," Jeremy said.

"No," Emma replied. "I think the Twelve Days of Murder would be better. There's more than one murder for three French hens."

"That's true," he acknowledged.

"What the hell are you two talking about?" Ennis asked.

"We could be clearer," Cole said with a quick glare at Emma and Jeremy. He went on to explain. "Someone is using the song to set up murders for each night."

Ennis shook his head. "I'm sorry, I'll need an example."

Frank said, "For five golden rings, the rings were found on five fingers in some soup at a restaurant."

Ennis's eyes went wide as he realized the implications. "Jayzus, ten piper's piping! How close are we?"

"Very close. Just two days."

"But... but," he stammered, "that's when we're having the event."

"It lines up, and that's why we're here," Cole said.

Ennis stood in agitation. "And all the pipers that're in the area will be making their way here. And their families!"

"Yes," Frank admitted.

Ennis stood and walked to the fireplace, he turned back to them. "Do we need to cancel?"

"No, sir," Emma said. "I think it'll be more dangerous to do that. The murderer will still go after pipers, but if you're in one location, we can protect you."

"I don't want the men to come into this unawares."

"Are you planning any rehearsals?" Emma asked, drumming on her lips.

"We had to move it to tonight. The parade's tomorrow, and a lot of our members have kids." He stopped suddenly, eyes widened. "The parade! The drummers!"

"The police are covering them," Cole told him.

"Aren't you with the police?"

"No, sir," Jeremy said. "We're more like private detectives."

"I'll be there, too," Frank told his friend.

"Good."

"We're working with the task force," Cole explained. "They're concentrating on the parade. The chief asked them to get involved and give support on night ten."

"Can you be at the hall this evening?" Ennis asked.

"Who all will be there?" asked Jeremy.

"The pipers and their families. It'll be a social event as well as a rehearsal."

"We can bring Hen with us," Jeremy said to Emma.

"She'll enjoy that." Emma turned to Ennis. "Mr. Ennis, we'll bring sketches of the men who we believe are involved in this. That way, if they're spotted, we can head off anything from happening."

"You and your families are welcome. It's a potluck."

"We'll bring desserts. Speaking of which, we also need to go by that bakery on the way home," Emma told Jeremy.

"Oops," Jeremy remembered, "we have several people coming to the house tonight."

"Bring them, too," Ennis offered.

"We'll check with them and see if they'd like to come," Emma promised.

They stood and Frank said, "John, thanks for taking the time to listen to us."

"I want to keep my pipers and their families safe," he said simply. He wrote down the address and handed it to Cole. "We'll be there starting at six tonight."

"We'll be here," Frank replied.

Cole checked his watch; the driver would arrive soon. "Hen," called Jeremy.

She ran out with the boys, cookie crumbs around her mouth. Jeremy took out his handkerchief and wiped it gently. "Were the cookies good?"

"They were good. Almost as good as Dora's."

"You better not tell her that," he teased.

The older boy ran to the window and called out, "Papa, there's a carriage outside. Are we going somewhere?"

"No, silly, our company is headed home," Ennis told the boy. "Come on, boys, stand by me and tell them goodbye."

They did as they were told, waving goodbye and saying, "Bye." The baby grinned and waved.

The group waved back and then made their way into the cold weather; thankfully the wind had died down. They climbed into the carriage and traveled back to the police station to drop Frank off. "Thank you for accompanying us," Cole told the man.

"Thank you for involving me. I'll be at the hall tonight." He hesitated on his way out of the carriage. "Do we need to worry about tonight?"

"I don't think so," Jeremy replied. "The murders tend to happen in order on the day mentioned in the song." Frank nodded and stepped down and the carriage continued on.

"Let's head to the boarding house for lunch," suggested Emma.

"And we can ask the family if they'd like to go see the pipers tonight," Jeremy said.

"I want to go," Hen commented.

"You'll be with us," confirmed Jeremy. She smiled broadly.

Cole used his walking stick to tap the carriage roof, and the driver opened the small window above their heads. "Yes, sir?"

"We'd like to head back to the boarding house."

"Yes, sir," the driver said and closed the small door.

They arrived and went into the house; conversations could be heard coming from the dining room. "Sounds like lunch has been served," Jeremy observed. They stored their coats and hats and moved into the dining room.

"I hope you have extra," Cole said.

"You're welcome anytime, Cole," Ethyl told him. "It shouldn't be a problem." She called over her shoulder, "Amy, we need an extra plate."

Amy came through with a plate and stopped abruptly. When she didn't move, Dora said, "Amy, I think Cole needs the plate in front of him." She unfroze and put the plate in front of him. Neither said a word nor smiled. Amy turned and went back to the kitchen.

Emma sat next to Dora and whispered, "What's going on?"

"No idea. Looks like a fight," she muttered back. "Eat, everyone," Dora prompted. Trays were passed around and people ate their fill.

"How is the investigation going?" asked Tim.

"We think we have found the pipers," said Jeremy.

"Already?" asked Dora.

"What's a piper?" asked Patrick.

Cole answered. "Bagpipes, the piper blows into a pipe into bags. The sounds come from that."

"These men are professionals, from all over the country. In fact, there's an event tonight that we're invited to," Emma said tentatively.

Dora frowned. "We'd planned a party here tonight."

Cole spoke up. "You're all invited."

"Including Mom, Ellis, and Jake," Jeremy added.

"Ethyl and Amy also," Cole put in.

"It's a potluck," Emma told Dora.

"Hmmmm. A piper's event?" Dora said. "Well, it should be fun. We do have plenty of food to bring," She looked at Emma. "Baked goods are your responsibility, my dear."

"Going to get on that right after lunch," Emma promised.

"Are you going to the bakery?" Hen asked Emma.

"I am."

"Can I go with you?"

"Of course you can."

"I need to be in the office for a few hours this afternoon," Jeremy said to Emma.

"We can drop you off on the way."

After lunch they dropped off Jeremy and Cole at the Pinkerton office and then she and Hen headed to the bakery. "Emma..." Hen asked tentatively, looking down at her hands.

"What is it, baby?" Emma asked, watching the snow fall outside the window of the carriage.

"Family always works at the bakery, right?"

"That's right."

Hen kept her face down. "I'm family, aren't I?" she asked plaintively.

Emma turned to the girl and lifted her chin with her hand. "Oh, baby, of course you are."

"Then why haven't I been asked to work there?"

"We have several family businesses, Hen, and you've been

working at the foundation. The work you've done there is important."

"I'd like to work at the bakery, to be like the other cousins in the family," Hen said in a rush.

"Hmm," Emma said, "I think I can work that out. Did you want to try one day a week and still go to the foundation on the other days?"

"I'd like that. I want to get to know my family more."

"I'll talk to Cousin about the schedule after Christmas."

"If I like it, can I ask for more hours?"

"The bakery's hard work, often with heavy deadlines. Do you think you can manage that?"

"I want to try."

"How about this? You, Dora, and I practice some recipes for goodies over the next few weeks. Maybe Amy and Ethyl can help out, too."

"That will be great!" Hen grinned. "And when it's warmer can we start my self-defense classes again?"

"That's a definite yes."

"And can we practice knife throwing?"

"Well, I'm not sure about that one," Emma said cautiously.

"You learned when you were young," Hen reminded her.

"Who told you that?"

"Jeremy. And Grandpa Ellis. And Dora. And Tim…"

"Okay, okay. I get the picture. I was a bit older than you, though. Maybe in a few years."

"Maybe," Hen agreed.

"Right now, it's more important that you can protect yourself." Something had happened to Emma at a young age that nearly took her life. Papa worked hard to make sure she'd never feel helpless like that again. "Now, if I remember, the last thing we worked on was the sweeping kick, to knock the legs out from under an attacker. Have you been practicing?"

"Yeah. Only, Patrick won't let me practice with him anymore."

"Why not?"

"I knocked him on his butt one too many times."

She grinned. "I like hearing you're working on it."

The carriage pulled to a stop at the back of the bakery. They climbed out. "Do you want me to come back for you?" the driver asked.

"No thanks, we're waiting for Jeremy to come back for us."

"Great, that means I can get out of the snow!" the driver called back, and with a wave, he pulled away.

They walked into the small courtyard behind the bakery and approached the door. They entered quickly; the room was full of bakers in a double row of tables. Large fired ovens lined the back of the room. Emma's cousin, Frederick, walked around with a clipboard, confirming which orders were completed. His eyes drifted to Emma. "Here to work, I hope?" he asked.

"No, more of a pickup." She checked her watch. "Though, I do have a few hours to spare and Hen wants a chance to help out."

Cousin tapped his clipboard slowly. "She's family. It's where she belongs." Hen grinned as Emma teared up a bit; she loved her family. "Okay, you both move over there. We have several batches of cookies to get out."

Emma looked at Hen. "Ready to learn to make cookies?"

"Yes, please."

They moved to the table and removed their coats. "Go hang these in the closet." Hen took them and quickly hung them up. She rushed back. "Next, we wash our hands. We have to be clean while baking."

When they got back to their bench, Emma and Hen put on their aprons. Emma retrieved a large bowl from the shelves under the table. "Can you carry this?" asked Emma.

"I can," Hen said, taking it. When she didn't look strained, they walked to the supply shelves. Emma started calling out the ingredients needed to make the cookies and Hen began gathering the items.

Once the bowl and their arms were full, they moved back to the bench. Hen took on the role of stirring as the ingredients were added. Once all of the ingredients were combined, Emma showed her how to use a spoon to make balls to be placed on baking trays. They were prepared with butter and flour. An hour had passed, and the cookies started to come out of the oven.

"Don't touch," Emma said. "These will be hot, and we need to move them to cool on the table. Work carefully—we need the shapes to stay as uniform as possible." Hen listened and performed the task carefully. Once the cookies had been moved off and were cooling, Emma asked, "Want one?"

"Can I?"

"They're your first cookies. Taste one." Hen looked carefully and picked one up. She took a large bite and chewed. "Is it good?" asked Emma.

"Yeah, it is."

"You're sure you want to work here?"

"I do."

"Then give me a few minutes and I'll talk to Cousin for you."

"I'll wait here," Hen promised.

"Why don't you start putting the boxes together? They're over there," Emma said, pointing to the end of the table.

"How many?"

She checked the list on their workstation. "Looks like twelve, a dozen each." She left her to work on the boxes and went to find Cousin. "Martha," she called to the baker at the next table. "Where's Cousin?"

"In his office as usual." Martha pointed.

Emma entered the office and saw the desk was covered with papers and the filing cabinets overflowed behind him.

"Emma, did you need something?" he asked.

"Busy?"

"It's Christmas. It's always busy." He smiled. He could see something was on his cousin's mind and looked at her expectantly.

"Hen asked me to talk to you."

"What about?" he asked, though he was fairly certain he knew.

"She'd like to do what other family members are doing by working at the bakery."

He grinned and sat back. "She's family now; it should be expected that she'd put in her time here."

Emma grinned. "Thank you."

"For what? I could use a good baker."

"She'll need to apprentice for a while."

He shook his head. "What? You think I don't know how to bring in a new baker? Leave it to me."

"I will. When would you like her to start?"

"If you want, you can drop her off early in the morning. That way, she can learn how to set up for the day."

"I'll drop her off myself."

Cousin squinted his eyes. "Going to do any more baking for me?"

"Not now," she said with regret. "We have a case that's taking up my time." She stood and headed toward the door.

Cousin called out. "Don't forget to pick up Dora's order!"

"I'm heading to get it now." She left the office and headed to the pick-up station; the items meant for them were marked with their name. She gathered them up and took them to their worktable.

The boxes were assembled and piled high next to the cookies. "You did a good job," Emma said. "Now, we fill each one. Be careful not to break any. Watch me." She filled the box carefully and closed it.

"Can I do the next one?" Hen asked.

"Yes." Emma watched the girl fill the box carefully and, when it closed, she said, "Keep going, same method." Once the boxes were filled, Emma continued. "Each will have twine tied into a bow." They worked on the boxes and, when completed, Emma and Hen moved them to the pick-up table. "Cousin," Emma called, "we're done."

He walked out. "Thanks for helping out." He looked around. "I don't see Jeremy, so I guess you can bake some more."

At that moment, the back door flew open and hit the wall. Jeremy walked in and got shouted out at from all sides of the bakery. "Close the door!" He pushed the door closed and walked over to Hen. "Whew, windy out there. Ready to go?" he asked.

"We are." Hen and Emma gathered up the baked goods.

"Wait," Cousin said, "you must take a box of your cookies with you, Hen." He handed them to her. She grinned brightly and held them tight.

"Did you bake today?" Jeremy asked.

"I did!"

"Wow. Good for you. I can't wait to taste them," he said. Her grin got wider. He took the boxes from them and said, "After you." They walked ahead of him to the door. There was some struggle with the wind, but they finally made it outside, baked goods intact.

The carriage driver had waited for them. They climbed in and he quickly pulled out, so quickly that they were thrown together. "Guess he wants to get out of the weather," Jeremy grumbled. They made it home in a short time, and the driver left them standing on the sidewalk in front of the house as he rushed away.

"Guess he *really* wants to get out of the weather," Hen deadpanned.

"All right, upstairs," Emma said. The trio carried everything inside.

NOTEBOOK MYSTERIES ~ THE TWELVE DAYS OF MURDER

Amy met them in the foyer. "Did you pick up everything for me?"

"I got everything," Emma confirmed.

"Bring them into the kitchen. We're arranging everything to take to the potluck." They followed her and laid the items down on the round kitchen table. "Don't unpack anything," ordered Amy. "We'll put them as they are into the box to take with us." She checked each one. "Wait, there's an extra box of cookies. Dora didn't request these."

Hen stood taller. "I made those," she said proudly.

Amy looked at the box and then at the girl. "You did? I'll have to try one."

"Beat you to it," Jeremy snickered. He'd gone behind Amy and snuck a cookie.

"Oh, you," she huffed. "Out now, we have work to do."

Jeremy scarfed the cookie in three bites. "Hen, that was a good cookie."

"I'm glad you liked it."

They walked into the sitting room and dropped down onto the sofa. "Hen, tell Jeremy about the bakery," Emma encouraged.

Hen turned to Jeremy. "It was such fun! I got to make cookies. Well, I got to help make cookies."

"Soon, you'll be doing it on your own," Emma assured her. Jeremy frowned at that. "Hen asked if she could work like the other cousins at the bakery."

"Is that something you want to do?" he asked Hen, his frown still in place.

"It is. I want to start soon."

Emma laughed. "Well, they want you in the morning as an apprentice. Is that soon enough?" she teased.

"Oh, that's great. But what will I wear?" Hen remembered that the other girls wore all-white dresses with white aprons. She wanted to be just like them.

"Don't worry, I have just the thing," Emma told her. "Do you want to go upstairs and try on one of my bakery outfits?"

"Yes, please."

"Why don't you run up and meet me in my room. I'll be up in a few minutes."

She and Jeremy watched her run up the stairs. As she stood up, Jeremy took her arm. "Emma, I'm worried we're having her work too much. She needs to be a kid more."

"Jeremy, she asked for it and she sees that her new family has traditions, and she wants to be part of it." He continued to frown. She reached over and smoothed his frown lines. "Look, if it turns out to be too much, we'll slow down on going to Claire's office."

"All right," he said finally, "but I still don't like it."

Hen leaned over the banister and called down. "Emma, are you coming up?"

"On my way," Emma called back. "Do you want to come up?" she asked Jeremy.

"No, I will stay down here and read."

She smiled slightly and looked up as Hen called again. "I need to go up."

"Go on."

She went up and met Hen at the door. "Ready?" she asked.

"Ready!"

They went in. The bedroom was neat, and Jeremy's door was closed. Hen sat on the bed with a bounce. Emma walked to the closet and pulled out her white bakery dress.

"Oh, Emma, it's so pretty," Hen exclaimed.

"It might be just the right length for you." Emma had worn her dresses shorter than the other girls. "Take off your dress."

Hen followed the directions, slipped off her dress, and laid it on the bed. Emma helped her step into the other dress. Hen slid her arms into the sleeves and pulled it up. Emma stood behind her and buttoned her up. She tied the ribbon on the back and said, "Turn around and let me see how it fits."

Hen turned and Emma looked at the dress with a critical eye. "The length's good. You're a little smaller in the shoulders and the sleeves are a little long."

"Oh no! Will it stop me from going in tomorrow?"

"No," she said decisively, glancing at the clock. "We have time. Let's move up to the sewing room."

CHAPTER 9

*T*he evening hour came quickly.

Outside, Emma and Jeremy stood at the carriage while everyone donned their coats. Jeremy looked down the street. "Is that Pops?" he asked. "Who's that with him?"

Emma knew the answer without looking, but she peered toward them. "Yeah, that's Cole and… um… Amy."

"Are they… Are they fighting?"

Emma glanced their way again. "Um… Looks like."

"But why would they be fighting out in the cold?" he asked confused.

She sighed. "I'm not sure what the fight is about, but it's time you knew. Amy and Cole have been dating each other. They have been for a while."

Jeremy was still confused, and he shook his head. "Pops and Amy? But he hasn't mentioned it. Did it just happen?"

"No, it's been going on for a long while now. Since before Paris even."

"Before Paris!" He turned to her. "And how long have you known?" he accused.

"Almost since the beginning."

"And you didn't tell me?"

"I didn't tell you because you get all…" She faltered.

"All what?"

"You know. You get all you."

"Huh. Yeah, I guess I do."

"Besides, they wanted privacy, and they weren't ready to tell anyone."

"Then how come you know?"

"I notice things, remember? And Dora works with Amy every day."

"Dora knows? Is that all?"

"If Dora knows, then Tim knows. Oh, Abbey knows."

"Mom knows, too? Anyone else?"

"Hmmm. Maybe Papa. Abbey tells him everything."

"Why didn't I notice?"

"Because you're you." She took pity on him when she saw the look on his face and simply said, "He's your dad."

"Were you ever going to tell me?"

"I'd hoped they'd tell you, but from the looks of that fight, it may be over." They watched Amy shake her head and storm off.

"You're right," Jeremy said, watching his father walk to the back of the house, his head hung low. "I'll keep my mouth shut."

"Probably for the best."

The family started to walk down the stoop. The kids would ride in the carriage with Dora, Ethyl, and Amy. The rest would ride in a wagon with the food. Abbey and Ellis would pick up Jake and meet them there. Once everyone was loaded in, they huddled down and travelled to the party.

When they got there, there was already a long line of wagons and carriages dropping people off.

"This is only the rehearsal?" Cole asked in surprise. "If this is just the rehearsal, then there will be a lot of people to manage on the night of the event."

"Not all of these are the pipers," commented Jeremy.

"We'll meet the group inside," Emma said.

Everyone grabbed a dish or baked goods and walked in. Jeremy hung back with Emma. "Pops and Amy are avoiding each other."

"Leave it alone," she said firmly.

He nodded and they walked into the building. "Emma, Jeremy!" They looked over and saw Frank striding towards them.

"Hi, Frank, pipers all here yet?"

"They're getting here. We should be able to meet with them once people start eating." He looked at what they were carrying. "Can I help with that?"

"Please," Emma said, handing over the dish she was carrying. The group made their way to a table and started settling in. Dora and Amy had joined the ladies in organizing the food.

The flow of people lessened, and John Ennis stood and asked everyone to bow for a prayer. Afterwards, he said, "Everyone get some food. We'll start the rehearsal after."

A line formed at the table. Frank tapped Emma and Jeremy on the shoulder, beckoning them to follow. She waved to Cole, who was staring at Amy. "Cole!" she called. He noticed her and walked over; they went to the stage area at the far end of the large space. Ennis spotted them and waved them up. Once they were on stage, he said to his group, "Boyos, this is Emma Evans, Cole, and Jeremy Tilden, and of course you all know Frank."

The men nodded and called out, "Hello."

Ennis started. "I've told the men about what we'll be facing on the night of the concert."

"Will our families be safe here?" called one.

"Should we cancel?" called another.

Frank stepped up. "Gentlemen, you know me. I brought my own family here tonight. These people who're here to help us brought their families. Please, listen to them."

Cole approached. "We feel it'll be safer to have you in one

place. We'll have Pinkerton detectives undercover, some even up on the stage with you."

That caused some laughter. "Will they be able to pipe?"

"They'll hold the pipes and, if you could give a little guidance, it would be appreciated."

Emma nodded. "We have these handouts for you. These are the two men we'll need to watch for." She took them to Ennis, and he passed them around. "We'd appreciate it if you could keep this quiet. The less publicity on this, the better."

"Can we talk for a moment?" Ennis asked.

The four stepped away to give them privacy. It was only a few moments before Ennis called them back. "We've agreed as a group that being together is safer. We'll work with you."

"Great," Jeremy said. "Cole and I met with several of our detectives, and they're here tonight." Jeremy waved toward the crowd and two detectives approached, Garrison and Kelly. "These men will stay with you tonight and then on the day of the concert. The day of the event, we'd prefer if you stayed at your homes until you come here."

Garrison and Kelly walked to the stage and took the chairs Ennis indicated. They were handed pipes and the men around them showed them how to hold them.

Frank turned to Emma, Jeremy, and Cole. "Go get something to eat. I'll stay up here."

"He wants to take notes," Ennis told them.

"Notes for what?" asked Emma.

"He collects tunes."

"I want to record music, so it doesn't get lost," Frank explained. "Maybe one day I'll publish a book."

One of the men called, "Ah, put the pen down and bring your flute up here."

Frank pulled a case out of his jacket. "You mean this?" The men laughed and got him a chair.

"Let's leave them to it," Jeremy said and the three walked to the table to get some food. There was a large assortment. It all looked good. They filled their plates and sat down. The music started and stopped a few times, the men finding their rhythm. It was a rehearsal as well as a get together. Once the music started, people began to dance and enjoy the night.

Cole sat at the far end of a long table. Amy was at the other end. "Hey, Pops, everything okay?" Jeremy asked his dad.

"Yes, of course," Cole replied, picking up his fork.

Jeremy looked over at Emma and she shook her head in warning. He decided to let it go.

Hen came and got Jeremy out onto the dance floor. Everyone had a marvelous time. When it looked to be going late into the evening, Emma said, "I need to get Hen home. She has the bakery in the morning."

"Pops, we need to get Hen home."

"Go ahead. I'll make sure the rest of the family gets home."

They waved to Frank; he'd had a flute to his mouth most of the night. Hen fell asleep in the carriage on the ride home. "Did we keep her out too late?" asked Jeremy.

"She'll be fine. She'll only be there for about three hours tomorrow and she can nap after."

CHAPTER 10

❦

$\mathcal{T}$he ninth Day of Christmas

The next morning, Emma went to Hen's room and knocked on her door. It swung open quickly and Hen was standing in the doorway in her white dress. She turned and moved her hair out of the way. "Can you button me up?"

Emma laughed. "I thought I'd have to wake you up."

"No, I'm ready now."

"Then let's go down; the carriage should be here soon." They walked downstairs and into the kitchen. A note sat out from Dora. It said Hen's lunch was in the ice box and to take an apple. "You know she used to leave the same notes for me," Emma told the girl.

"Really?" Hen asked. She wanted to be just like her family. They packed her lunch and apple, and they walked to the door. The carriage stood outside.

"Coats," Emma reminded her. They bundled up quickly and

headed outside to the waiting carriage. Emma called the address up to the driver and got Hen inside quickly.

"Remember to follow directions today and be polite," Emma reminded her.

"I will," Hen promised.

At the bakery, Hen settled in quickly and Emma looked at the pastries on the table. "Cousin, can I take a few this morning?"

"Of course."

She kissed Hen. "I'll be back for you later. I love you."

"Okay. I love you, too." Hen had already been assigned to another baker, one of her many cousins.

Emma put the pastry in a bag. *This is for Mark*, she thought.

The carriage had waited and took her back home. It was still early, but she went to Mark's boarding house and used a hidden key to get in.

Emma rushed upstairs and bumped into an older woman coming from the opposite direction. "I'm sorry," said Emma.

The woman mumbled a reply. Emma turned and got a good look at her. "You!" It was Coreen Harden, John Harden's mother. When she and Emma had last met, she'd tried to stab Emma in the neck with a pair of knitting needles.

"It's me," Coreen grunted, her face set in firm lines.

"What the hell are you doing here? Around my family?"

"That, young lady, is none of your business."

Emma stepped toward her menacingly. "Look, lady, anything affecting my family affects me."

"Why don't we take this downstairs?"

"Why? Got some knitting needles with you again?" When Coreen glared at her, Emma said, "After you." Her words belayed her mood.

"No, please, after you," Coreen said sweetly.

Emma turned and went down the stairs. As she stepped one booted foot onto the floor, she felt something land on her back and fists begin beating the back of her head. "Ow, shit!" Emma howled in anger. "Old woman, you get on my last nerves!" Emma grabbed the woman's shoulders and flipped her over onto the floor and sat on her chest.

"All right, old woman, why are you in this house?"

"Still ain't none of your business," Coreen huffed as she squirmed, trying to get Emma off of her.

"Need any help there?" Jeremy asked from the doorway. He'd been watching for Emma to get home and had seen the attack.

"Nah, I'm good."

"You might let her up," he suggested.

"Hey, she attacked me first. She jumped on my back and started beating the hell out of me."

He raised his eyebrows and got a good look at who it was. He whistled in amazement. "That's John Harden's mom?"

"It is," Emma said shortly. "If I let you up, will you be calm?" she asked Coreen.

"Fine," Coreen huffed. Emma got off of her with a hand from Jeremy. Emma turned toward her and the woman balled up her fist and swung it at her face. Jeremy reached out and blocked the punch.

"Hey, now," he admonished. "You agreed to be calm."

"Yeah, well, I just thought I owed her one last hit."

Suddenly, a cry rang out. Jeremy looked up the stairs. "Who's that with you?"

"My great-granddaughter."

"The one…" he started.

"Yeah, the one you rescued."

"Can I go up to see her?" he asked eagerly.

Coreen's face softened for the first time, and she said, "Well, you're her godfather."

He grinned broadly. "I am?"

"Yes. Go on up now and see her." He didn't wait and ran upstairs.

"Wait," called Emma and threw the pastry bag at him. "Give these to Mark." He grabbed the bag and started upstairs.

Emma looked at her. "You ready to talk?"

She sighed. "Sure. I guess I owe you that." They moved into the sitting room.

"Why are you here?"

"I moved first with the baby; her parents are following. John's setting up a house for us."

"Why now?"

"Rumblings of things coming. John wants us close. They can use the family as a weapon against him."

"When are these rumbling expected?"

"I'm not sure," Coreen said noncommittally.

"How did you end up here? Do Dora and Tim know who you are?"

"They do. John set it up with them. The baby's safety was the reason they agreed."

A gurgling sound came from the stairs as Jeremy descended with a happy little girl. "Look at all the curls," he said.

"Looks like she took to you right away," Coreen said. She made no moves to take her from him.

"She looks healthy and happy," commented Emma.

"She is, until nighttime approaches," Coreen muttered. "Then the noise sets in. That young lady's stubborn and misses her parents."

"Will they be here before Christmas?" Jeremy asked, holding up his watch for her to play with.

"That's the plan. They'll stay here until after the holidays."

"So, John will be spending Christmas here?" Emma asked slowly.

"Yeah, you got a problem with that?" Coreen asked menacingly.

"Now, don't start that again," Jeremy cautioned. "You're both strong women, but I don't think baby needs to see that."

"You right," they both begrudgingly agreed.

"Would you mind if I stay a while?" Jeremy asked them.

"I'd appreciate it," Coreen replied. "Would you mind if I took a nap?"

"Let me take her next store, that way she won't disturb you."

"Thank you," she said and started upstairs.

He called, "What's her name?"

"Jemma," she called back.

Jeremy barked a laugh. "I bet that got John's goat." He could hear Coreen laughing up the stairs.

Jeremy took his coat and wrapped it around the baby for the short walk. They entered the boarding house and saw the household was already awake. "Everyone, this is Jemma," he introduced the baby.

Dora came down the stairs with Tim and Lottie. "Is that the baby staying next store?" she asked.

"Yes," said Emma with a look at Dora.

"So, now you know."

"That you can also keep secrets," Emma teased her sister, "yes."

"How did your meeting with Coreen go?" Dora asked hesitantly.

"Oh, there was a fight," Jeremy said.

"A fight?" Dora said faintly.

"Oh yeah," he exclaimed. "A real dustup. Fists flying, furniture smashing, bones breaking, blood flowing. It was good times."

"Oh, hush, you muttonhead. It was nothing," Emma assured her sister. "There were just some past hard feelings that needed to be worked out."

"But she's just an old woman."

"One that can still pack a punch," Jeremy said gleefully.

CHAPTER 11

At the parade that evening

The parade started with a large band. Emma had her hands on Hen's shoulders. "Emma, you're holding too tight," Hen complained above the crowd noise.

"Sorry, baby," Emma said, loosening her hold.

Jeremy scanned the moving band in front of them. "The drums are coming up." He could see the officers walking with each group.

"I know the police are in charge," she reminded him. She was doing the same thing he was, monitoring the groups in front of them. There was a break between the bands with cars full of politicians. Hen waved to them enthusiastically. "Hey! It's Mark and Enzo! They're with the mayor!" The duo saw them and began waving enthusiastically.

"Well, I'll be damned," Jeremy said admiringly watching them go by. "Those two are heroes."

The next band approached. Hen frowned at a dark-haired

man in a hat that covered his ears. It was Griff, one of the men who had stolen the geese. He was walking close to the line of drummers. *That's one of the bad guys,* she thought. "Emma! Jeremy! Bad guy," she said, pointing to the man.

"What?" Emma asked. Her hearing was muted. Hen pointed again. Emma saw who she was pointing to and nudged Jeremy. "Jeremy," she whispered. He saw and started after him. "No, wait." Emma quickly unwrapped her long wool scarf. "Hen, come with me," she directed.

Jeremy caught on and said, "Right behind you."

Jeremy grabbed one end of the scarf and Emma the other. The man wasn't watching his path; his concentration was on the drummers. Hen ran out and did a sweeping kick, and he fell hard. Emma and Jeremy wrapped him in the scarf. The officer walking alongside picked him up and moved him away with little fuss.

"Do we go with them?" asked Hen.

"Nope," said Emma with a wide smile. "We stay and enjoy the parade." The crowd laughed at the clowns running by and cheered for the bands that seemed to be nonstop. The last wagons had people throwing candy and gifts. Emma held onto Hen. "But I want some," the girl protested.

"Not in that crush," Emma replied.

"I'll get you some," Jeremy said and dove into the crowd. He came back with several pieces of hard candy. "Here you go," he said, handing it to Hen. Hen giggled. Emma laughed. "What?" he asked.

"Your hair's sticking up," Emma said and patted it back down.

"Better now?" Jeremy asked Hen and Emma. They nodded.

CHAPTER 12

❦

The tenth day of Christmas; the next morning at breakfast

"Hen, you were a hero," Dora exclaimed.

"It wasn't just me. Emma and Jeremy helped."

The group laughed. "Are you two going into the station this morning?" Dora asked Emma and Jeremy.

"Yeah, we want to see what the man said when questioned."

"You'll be disappointed," a voice said behind them.

"Pops! I didn't know we were meeting here this morning," Jeremy said.

"I stopped by to let you know what happened after the man was taken into custody last night." They could tell he was serious. Emma and Jeremy stood and followed him to the study.

"We'll hold your breakfast," Dora called to them.

Once they were in the study, Cole looked to Jeremy. "Son, close the doors, please." He did as he was asked and walked back over to Cole. "The man didn't make it to the station last night," Cole said bluntly.

"What does that mean?" Emma asked.

"He was murdered. His body was found in the wagon."

"Who had access to him?"

"There was a lot of confusion, and the office who had secured him got called away. There were about fifteen minutes where he was locked up and not being watched."

"Do you think it was the mole we suspect?"

"It's possible," Cole admitted.

"He was our chance to end this," Emma said miserably. "I thought we'd stopped this, or at least found out who else was involved. What do we do now?"

"Continue with our protection of the pipers, dancers, and lords," Jeremy told her.

"Yeah, you're right."

"There's a complication," Cole brought up. "All of the police focus will now be on the piper's."

"Will they interfere with our plans?" Jeremy asked.

"Wait a second," Emma said. "That also exposes our plan to the mole in the police department."

"I'll ensure that they're covering outside and the Pinkertons take care of the inside," Cole remarked.

"And if Coleman doesn't agree?" asked Jeremy.

"The chief will have to get involved," Emma said simply. "So, we're on tonight."

"We are," they agreed.

"Back to breakfast?" Jeremy asked.

"Yes," she turned to Cole. "Care to join us?"

"No, I don't think I will this morning." He walked to the foyer with them. "Jeremy, I'll be in the office."

"I'll come with you, Pops."

"Meet me outside; the carriage is waiting."

"He's avoiding Amy," Emma said.

"Yeah," he replied, staring toward the door his father had exited through.

"You gonna ask him about it?"

"I'm thinking about it," he said, kissing her quickly and walking out the door.

"Eat something!" she called.

"Thanks, Mom!"

Emma smiled and walked into the dining room and stopped suddenly. "Savannah, Ethan!" she exclaimed. "What're you doing here?"

"What, we get married, and we can't we come back?" Savannah teased her friend.

"Banished for Christmas," murmured Ethan.

"No, of course not. I thought you were both at your other house through the holidays."

"We love it there," confirmed Savannah. Ethan nodded. "But I was called into work for a show. The stage manager has gone out sick."

"I'm sorry you had to come off vacation."

She shrugged. "It'll be fun to be at the theatre at Christmas."

Emma had a sudden thought. "Dora, where's the newspaper?" she asked.

"Check the kitchen," Dora suggested. Emma went through the door to retrieve the paper. "What're you looking for?" she called.

"Dancer's dancing," Emma said and walked back into the dining room with the papers. "Does anyone have events tomorrow night involving dancers?"

"We do," Savannah volunteered. "Tomorrow at McVicker's Theater. It's a special performance involving local kids."

"Kids," Emma muttered. They'd blocked the murderer from killing after five gold rings. *Will he go after kids?*

"Yes. The kids have been working hard. We have rehearsals today."

Emma put down her paper. "That must be it."

"Tell me what's going on and why you're asking about the

kids?" Emma explained the twelve days of Christmas and the murders. Savannah's face paled. "But there're just kids! Do you think he'll go after them?"

"I think it's possible, yes."

"Then we need the police at the theatre."

"We'll have protection there," Emma confirmed. "Right now, we need to let the police know what we think."

"Ethan," Savannah asked, "can you come to the theatre with me?"

"Of course, I'll be there," he confirmed. "Is there anything or anyone I should be looking for?" he asked Emma.

"If there's anyone you don't know, especially on the crew, report them. Find out who they are and what they're doing there."

"Got it."

"How soon can you be there?" Savannah asked. She was gripping her napkin, her knuckles showing white.

"I'll head over to the Pinkertons now and get with Cole before we go over to the station."

"Will we be safe?"

"At least until the night of the dance. He likes to wait until the actual day so I'd expect something to be planned during the event."

"When the kids are dancing," Savannah said, her eyes wide.

"Yes."

She took a shuttering breath. "Okay. Come by as soon as you can."

Emma stood to leave. "Emma," called Dora.

She turned back to her sister. "Yes?"

"You haven't eaten."

"Oh, right!" She walked back to the table, sat, and filled her plate quickly.

"Slower, please, you have time," Dora said, taking a drink of her coffee.

"Okay, Mom," Emma said, grinning, but continued to eat fast. She laid her fork down picked up her plate and took it to the kitchen. She left it with Ethyl and returned to the dining room. She kissed Dora on the head and rubbed Lottie's brown curls. "I'm out now."

"Need a ride?" Tim asked.

"I do."

"I'm headed to get the wagon; I have some shopping to pick up this morning."

"Can we go out soon?" she asked, glancing at her watch.

"We can." Tim turned and called out, "Patrick! Emma wants to leave early."

Patrick walked out of the study. "I'm ready." Dora walked into the foyer with Lottie to inspect her family.

"Coats, hats, and mufflers."

"Yes, Mom," said Patrick.

"Yes, Mom," Tim added.

"Yes, Mom," Emma put in. Patrick laughed loudly at that, doubling over.

"All right, it wasn't that funny," Dora said.

"Yeah, it kind of was," Emma said with a smirk. They did as they were told and got their coats, hats, and mufflers in place. Dora did a final inspection.

"Don't stay out too long." She wagged her finger at all of them.

"Yes, ma'am," they replied together and exited the house into the cold.

"Brr." Patrick shivered.

"We'll get the wagon and drop off Emma at the Pinkerton's office first," Tim said.

They walked quickly toward the barn that held the wagon and horse. Once there, they took Emma over to the Pinkerton's office. She waved them off and went up the stoop into the office. Kelly was sitting at his desk. "He's in the office."

"Jeremy?"

"And Cole," he confirmed.

She started toward the office and turned to the man. "Thanks for helping out with the pipers."

He shrugged. "It was fun to sit in with them."

"The concert's tonight."

"Garrison and I'll be there," he confirmed.

She walked into Jeremy's office and found him and Cole staring at a board. It was identical to the one at the station.

"Emma, what you're doing here?" Cole asked.

"I came about dancer's dancing."

Jeremy asked, "Did you figure something out?"

"Savannah and Ethan were visiting." They waited expectantly for her to finish. "She has a dance show with local kids on the eleventh night."

"Kids," Jeremy gasped, dropping into his chair.

"And it's a large cast."

"Lots of people to watch."

"Do we go to the police?" Emma asked Cole.

Cole nodded. "We have to. They need to know about this. Like the piper's event, we could use their support, at least outside." Coats were gathered and they went into the front area.

"Kelly," Jeremy called.

"You called?" he asked.

"Could you get our carriage and driver? We need to go to the station and then McVicker's Theater."

"Going to watch a show?" he asked drolly.

"No, we're thinking it's the dancer's dancing," Emma told him.

"Oh," Kelly replied, recognition dawning on this face. "I'll go right now and take care of that."

They pulled on their coats and headed out front to the waiting carriage. Kelly was already inside. The carriage took them to the station. "When should I come back for you?" the driver asked.

"Wait, please. And, Kelly, wait with him," Cole replied. "I don't think we'll be long."

The clerk saw them come in the doors. "Bill's in the back and he is NOT in a good mood."

"Noted," Jeremy said grimly. Cole led the way to the situation room. Coleman stood at the front of the crowded room, talking about dancers dancing. Several theories were on the board, different balls, and events around town.

"They don't have the kids at McVicker's on the list," observed Emma.

"Then we bring it up," Jeremy responded. He raised his voice so he could be heard over the noise. "What about McVicker's Theater? They have a kid's show that night."

Coleman's mouth tightened. "The song says Lady's Dancing, not kids."

"Hey, that's right," Davies said. "We have ideas also, you know!"

"But with kid's getting hurt, the impact will be worse," Emma appealed.

Coleman had had enough of these consultants. "Look, if you think that, then you and the Pinkertons follow up on that lead. We'll be following up on '**Ladies** Dancing.'"

"We're getting nowhere with him," Cole told Jeremy and Emma. "We'll manage the theatre tomorrow night by ourselves. Let's go follow our lead."

They went out and joined Kelly in the carriage. "Is there a way to limit who'll be there?" Kelly asked.

"I don't think so," Emma replied. "It's a family event. So, I assume there'll be lots of family members there."

"What about the crew?" Jeremy asked. "We could limit the access where the kids are located?"

"We'll have to talk to Savannah about that," Emma said.

The carriage pulled to a stop in front of the theatre. "Come back in a few hours, please, Jerry," Cole told the driver. He nodded and, after they disembarked, he pulled away.

They entered the large theatre. The foyer was dark red, with a carpeted floor and painted walls. Gold accents on the banisters lead up staircases ascending to both the left and right.

"How do we get backstage?" Emma asked, looking around.

"I can show you," said a pretty little girl standing nearby. She was in a pink tutu and a large pink bow in her red hair.

"Do you have someone with you?" Emma asked.

"No, we're just hanging out, waiting for the rehearsal to start."

Jeremy muttered, "That's the first thing we gotta correct."

"We can get Claire and Thomas to help out with this," Emma said.

"That's a good idea," Cole agreed.

Emma asked the little girl, "Can you take us backstage?"

"Sure. Follow me." She led them to the left to a dark door. She opened it and it led to a long hallway. As soon as they left the main floor, the areas looked more worn. *No reason for extras back here*, Emma thought.

Jeremy looked around. "Anyone can get in here. We should put someone on that door." Cole nodded his agreement.

The little ballerina continued down the hallway, past different rooms with children in each one. The girls shouted a "Hello" as they went by. They walked around the racks of costumes in the hallways. At the stage, she turned to them and said, "Here you go."

"Thank you," said Emma.

"No problem." The girl ran off.

"Emma!" they heard Savannah call. They turned toward her as she ran over to them. "Thank you for coming."

"Savannah, this is Kelly," Jeremy introduced the detective.

"Nice to meet you," she said.

NOTEBOOK MYSTERIES ~ THE TWELVE DAYS OF MURDER

"Is there somewhere we can discuss things?" Cole asked her.

"Yes, this way. The stage manager's office is just off the stage." They followed her into the office. Once the door was closed, she turned to them and asked, "What can we do to protect the kids?"

"We have some ideas," Jeremy began. "Additional security and keeping the kids in one location with guardians would be a start."

"We usually let the kids have the run of the place," Savannah told him, "but we can make that work. What's this about additional security?"

Emma said, "The backstage doors aren't secure and anyone who knows that can walk in anytime."

"We haven't had any problems before, but I get that. We'd need locks added. I'm not sure we have anyone to guard the doors."

"We can provide the men," Cole told her.

"Good. When do you want to make the changes?"

"Today."

Kelly spoke up. "We'll need a full tour to make sure we have all of the areas covered."

Emma drummed her fingers on her lips. "The crew, how are they managed?"

"They work directly for the theatre, though we sometimes have traveling tours that come through with their own crew."

"Do you know everyone for this show?"

"No, not really," Savannah admitted. "Most of the people working this event are volunteering."

Cole looked at Jeremy. "We'll need to interview all of the crew."

"We'll need to know what previous shows they've worked," Jeremy confirmed.

Savannah sighed and asked, "Do we have time to get all of this organized?"

"We'll make time," Cole promised. He turned to Kelly. "Get word out to the men, tell them this involves kids and, if they're in town, all vacations should be put on hold for tomorrow night."

"They won't hesitate and most are in town."

"Great, can you go now?"

"I'll get a carriage back," Kelly said and left the room.

"What now?" asked Savannah.

"We need to tour the location," Jeremy replied. Savannah bit her lip.

"What's wrong?" asked Emma.

"We're starting rehearsals soon. Can I send someone with you?"

"Of course."

She opened the door and called, "Bobby!"

A young man ran over. "Savannah, we're almost ready to start."

"I know, I'll handle the rehearsals. I need you to take these people around and show them all of the exits and entrances and anything else they might want to see."

He frowned and asked, "Do we have time to be showing people around now? Can't they come back later?"

Cole started to talk and Savannah held up her hand to him. "Bobby, we have a possible security issue, and this show involves kids."

"Oh." He blinked. He handed Savannah the clipboard and said, "Please, follow me." They followed him out.

Savannah looked at the clipboard and started to write on it as she headed to start the rehearsals.

"Where would you like to start?" Bobby asked.

"How do people get in and out of the stage areas?" asked Emma.

"The long hallway by the changing rooms. There're a lot of side doors that go outside to move in sets and equipment."

"Do the actors use these doors?" Jeremy asked.

"They do. The public knows about them, too, because they wait for autographs there."

"Do these doors have locks?" Cole asked.

"Yeah, we lock the building before we leave." Bobby walked them to the five doors that were backstage. Cole documented the personnel that would be required for each one.

"The men will need to be dressed in black. That way, they're less likely to be seen," Bobby explained.

"Got it."

Emma looked around. "Is there a room where we can have all of the kids in one place?"

"The green room," Bobby said immediately.

"Green room?"

"It's a room near the stage where the actors can relax as they wait to go on stage."

"Is it big enough?"

"It is," he confirmed.

"Then we'll put them there."

Jeremy said, "We'll also need to confirm the guardian's names for each child before they're released to them."

"You know," said Cole, looking around, "we need the crew to sign in also so our guys can monitor them."

Emma stared up at the lights. "Are there people up there?"

"There are. They operate the lights from there."

"Can we go up and see them?"

"Let me get you a crew member who's familiar with that area." Bobby looked around and called, "Rick!"

A young man in dark clothes ran over, looking harried. "The rehearsals are about to start. What do you need?"

"This is important. I need you to take these people up to the lighting catwalks above the audience."

Cole interrupted. "Jeremy and Emma will go."

"They need to go up and view the lighting systems up there?" Rick asked. "Now?"

"Yes, now!"

"All right, follow me." Rick beckoned to Emma and Jeremy.

They followed him to the ladder, and he started up. Emma took her skirt from the back and tucked it in her front belt, making a quick set of pants. She started up with Jeremy close behind her. They stepped onto the narrow catwalk. Rick had moved over to the lighting system and waited for them.

"How do these work?" asked Emma.

"These are limelights and are spotlights. They're made up of a cylinder of lime and then we direct an oxyhydrogen flame onto it. A lens is then used to concentrate the light into a beam. We can adjust the burning calcium oxide. Our main job is to manage the two cylinders of gas, so we don't have a fire."

She noted that in her notebook. She and Jeremy looked around the area. "See anything?" she asked Jeremy.

"Nothing that jumps out at me, but I could be looking right at something and not know what it is, short of someone standing up and saying 'Hey, I'm the killer.'"

"Yeah, I agree," she told him. "How about you?" She turned to Rick. "Do you see anything that looks out of the ordinary?"

Rick looked around. "No," he admitted. "I was up here a little bit ago doing a lighting check and nothing looked out of place."

Emma nodded, then she and Jeremy followed the technician back down the ladder to finish their security tour.

CHAPTER 13

That night at the piper's event

The event was in full swing. The crowds were large, with both families and the public invited. It was an event that required tickets, and the profits would be donated to Irish causes and charities close to John Ennis' heart.

The tables had been scattered throughout with desserts and drinks being offered. Emma and Jeremy sat close to the stage, and there was an open area for dancing. She was concentrating on the pipers.

"What're you looking for?" he asked.

"I'm not looking, I'm counting the pipers. I just want to make sure we keep track of all of them."

He nodded and glanced around the room. The Pinkerton detectives were mixed in with the public. Their family weren't with them tonight, as they needed to concentrate on the job at hand.

"Wait." She counted again. "Someone's missing."

Jeremy looked over quickly and chuckled.

"What am I missing?"

"I believe that Piper's with Kelly."

"Why do you think that?"

"Garrison and Kelly have to go with them to the restroom."

"Oh, I guess that's important."

"With all the beer being drank, yes."

The evening flowed; the music was wonderful. Emma and Jeremy even got up and danced a jig. Out of breath, they sat back down and she went back to her counting. She grabbed his arm. "Jeremy, at least five pipers are missing."

He looked. Garrison and Kelly were still there. "What's going on?" The lights suddenly went out. "It looks like they're going after the pipers now! Let's go!"

Emma removed her knife from its hidden sheath and Jeremy pulled out his gun as they moved quickly to the stage in the dark. A light appeared to the right of the stage. "There!" he said, and they hurried toward it. When they got close to the light, Jeremy cocked his pistol and pointed it in the direction of the light. Emma kept her knife down but was ready to use it.

The main lights were turned up and they were suddenly face-to-face with the missing pipers. They were carrying a birthday cake, brightly lit with candles. The pipers gasped in surprise at the pistol pointed at them. Emma and Jeremy put away their weapons as unobtrusively as possible and moved out of the way. They watched the men carry the cake out on the stage to the grinning piper whose birthday it was.

Emma laughed suddenly, and Jeremy joined her. "Well, that was exciting," she said.

"It was," Jeremy agreed. "Hey," he said suddenly, "it's after midnight!"

"We made it, and the pipers are still safe." Emma let out a relieved breath.

Day ten down. Day eleven and the dancers were next.

CHAPTER 14

The eleventh night of Christmas; backstage at the McVicker's theatre

"Is everyone in place?" Cole asked.

"Yeah, everyone's at the doors. No one can get in unless they're approved," Kelly replied.

"I'm glad you guys are here," Savannah told Cole. "Are the police outside?"

"No, that's taken care of by us, too," said Jeremy.

"Especially since Bill doesn't agree with us," Emma muttered.

"They won't be here at all?" Savannah nervously.

"Let's just say that they have different theories and are covering other locations—dances and such. There're a lot of places that could fit dancers dancing; we could be wrong."

"Places," Savannah called and walked over to a group of girls.

"I don't think we're wrong," Jeremy said, looking around. "We're in the right area and kids dancing would have the largest impact."

"Shh," Bobby said from their left. "We're lifting the curtain."

The girls were all in place and standing stage right. Emma, Jeremy, and Cole moved out of the way as the girls lined up in their pink and white tutus. Several were giggling. Savannah held her finger to her lips. "Ladies, shhh." The girls quieted. The music swelled and the curtain lifted. Savannah tapped each girl on the back to tell them to go onstage.

They backed away and Cole whispered, "Do we think something will be dropped on them?"

"I'd be more fearful of a fire," Bobby whispered from behind them. "Remember the limelights. Each one has to be managed and monitored carefully."

"Are they being used for this show?"

"Right now, only the ones on the balconies. The catwalk should be empty during the performance. Unless a light goes out; then Rick or someone would go out to repair it."

They monitored the area and kept watch on the performing girls.

A light flashed from above. "Well, shit, what's going on up there?" Bobby exclaimed.

Jeremy and Emma looked up at the bright light. They ran toward the ladder. "What if it isn't something dropping but the fire that Bobby mentioned?" Jeremy said.

"Fire in a closed theatre?" Emma said. "That will kill more than just the dancers. People will trample each other to death trying to get out."

"All the more reason to get him." Jeremy climbed quickly with Emma right behind him. They stepped off onto the small platform and saw a man bent over the limelight lightbox. It was hard to sneak up on anyone on a structure that moved with each step.

Reed looked up at them. "Wait," Emma told Jeremy. "We don't want him to do something stupid." The man had a hand on the fire and a valve. "That's the hydrogen," Emma said. "Don't do that!" she called.

"I have to," Reed called back. "You don't know how he is. He'll kill me if I don't finish this."

"Yeah, well, we'll kill you if you do," she countered.

"He killed Griff when he got caught at the parade."

Jeremy tried to reason with him. "No, he died in custody."

"Exactly," Reed countered.

"Are you saying he's a policeman?" Jeremy asked.

Reed shook his head, his eyes wide, realizing he'd said too much.

"We gotta get to get him," Jeremy whispered to Emma.

"Knife?" she muttered.

"Can you get a good aim? If you miss, it could fall on the kids."

"No knife then."

Reed moved again, and the lightbox caught fire. They stopped talking and rushed him. Jeremy knocked him down and the platform rocked wildly. Emma reached down and pulled off her petticoat, which she covered over the small flame. There was some smoke, but the performance continued without interruption.

"Lose another petticoat?" Jeremy asked, holding Reed down with a knee in his back and his arms behind him.

"Yeah, at this rate, I won't have any left," she said. She remembered the instructions Rick had given her the day before and turned off the light. She turned the valve quickly.

Jeremy stood and pulled Reed up with him. "I can't go with you," Reed said in panic.

"You don't have a choice," Emma told him. Jeremy had Reed's arms behind his back, and he took off his tie and tied it around his hands.

Emma didn't want to wait and asked, "Which officer is it? Is it Coleman? Davies?"

Reed violently shook his head. "Noooo. I won't tell you! I can't!" He struggled with Jeremy and Emma. Instead of trying to run, he threw himself over the side. They looked over the railing. Reed was suspended from his wrists by the necktie.

"Let me go," he pleaded.

"But you'll die if you fall. Give me your hand!" Jeremy demanded.

Reed continued to struggle and appeared to be trying to climb back up when the tie tore and he fell backward. They ran quickly to the ladder and slid down with their hands to the ground and ran over to the man. Kelly was there. He looked up at them. "He didn't make it. It looks like the music was loud; no one heard him fall."

"Let's get him out of here before one of the kids sees him," Jeremy said.

Savannah came over and looked at the body. "Is it over?" she asked.

"The dancer's dancing seem to be safe," Emma told her.

"Good." Savannah went back to her program.

"Over here," Kelly called.

Several Pinkerton detectives came over, but another person Emma didn't expect was there, too. "Fred? Fred Smith? What're you doing here? I thought this was for Pinkertons only."

"It is, but I knew you had the right location. You're smarter than them."

"Get this man moved," Cole demanded. Fred pitched in and Reed's body was moved to the back and covered. The dance performance went on to a successful end.

Afterward, the theatre was empty, and they waited for the police. Yelling could be heard from outside. "Oh, joy. It's Bill," Jeremy said sarcastically.

"Oh, goody. I wonder what he'll say now that he was proven wrong," Emma commented.

"Again?"

"Again," she confirmed.

Coleman and Davies charged in. "What were you doing trying to apprehend the killer on your own?"

"Well gee, Bill, would you rather that the theatre had burned to the ground?" she snarled.

Coleman looked around. "No."

"Did you find any other issues at the other locations?" she asked innocently.

"Why should we tell you?" Davies snapped.

"No, we didn't find any other issues," Coleman admitted, ignoring Davies' outburst. "I hope this resolves night eleven. Thank you." Emma was surprised at the acknowledgment of their work. "Can you show me where he fell from?"

"I can," Jeremy said. He led Coleman over to the ladder.

"You think you're so smart," Davies fumed at Emma.

"Do I?" she asked. "We had a theory and followed through on it. Like any investigator."

"You're just a woman," Davies scoffed. "What do you know about investigating?"

Emma started to answer when Cole interrupted from behind her. "She knows more about investigating than you could ever learn. Why don't you get the hell out of our sight." It was not a question.

Emma smiled slightly as Davies stalked off.

"Want me to speak to McClaughry?" Cole asked her.

"It wouldn't do any good. He's just a little man. I don't mean he's short; he's just little in his brain and heart. Just like most men. He'll never see me, or any woman, as his equal or superior and that just proves he'll be little all his life." She looked over at Cole. "Well, the eleventh night's done."

"One more to go," he agreed.

CHAPTER 15

The twelfth night of Christmas

Carriages piled up outside at the Nickerson mansion on 40 East Erie Street. As they waited their turn, Emma leaned out the window, looking at the mansion. "That's a house? It looks like a museum."

"It does," Claire agreed. "It's called the Marble Palace. We'll go up those stairs. They curve into the entrance."

"There's also a floor under the first level," Thomas volunteered. They'd been to the home for several events.

"You're sure he'll be here?" Jeremy asked.

"Lord Brunsby?" asked Claire. "Oh, yes, he'll be here. I spoke to Sam Nickerson's secretary, and he confirmed the guest of honor would be here. Lord Brunsby loves a good party."

"He's actually a Duke," Thomas added, "the Duke of Lancaster. Lord is more of a generic name."

"Did Nickerson's secretary ask why you wanted to know?" Emma asked.

"He assumed I'd be asking Brunsby to contribute to the foundation."

"Are your men in place?" Thomas asked Jeremy.

"They are. The Pinkertons are working with the servers, and the police are handling the door and outside security," Emma replied for him.

"This is going to be the hardest event to keep track of," Jeremy commented. "All these people."

"And all those jewels and money in one room," Emma responded.

Claire laughed at that. "More than one room, I'm afraid. There are many rooms and many floors."

Their turn finally arrived, and the footman helped each person out of the carriage. They followed the other nicely dressed couples up the stairs. They stood in a line.

Emma looked at the brightly lit home. "I don't see any balconies."

"No," Jeremy agreed, staring at the house, "but there are lots of windows."

"So many," she said, disheartened. "How is this going to work?"

Claire studied the building. "There's a time when the more influential men will break away for some special brandy."

"How do you know?" asked Emma.

"It's kind of a tradition," she said.

"Okay, that might work."

"You think he'll work the room first to get the jewels? Harvey thought this was all just a scam," said Jeremy.

"If he's here for the money and the murders were just a distraction, do you think he'll even go forward with the lord's a leaping?" Claire asked.

Emma pondered that. "I think Harvey was right about the misdirection, but there's something more going on than just theft."

"What makes you say that?" Jeremy asked her.

"The level of commitment. It just seems odd that all this would end in a burglary. What if this IS about Lord Brunsby?"

The line moved and the men offered their elbows to the women to enter the front door. They entered and saw Kelly, dressed in a black suit and tie.

"Sir, Madam; invitation, please," he said, not acknowledging that he knew them.

"Yes, of course," Emma said, taking the invitation out of her purse.

Kelly looked at it and said, "Please, through that doorway. They'll take your coats there." They walked forward and heard him ask for an invitation from Thomas and Claire.

Once they were in the main foyer, the staircase dominated the room. Emma's eyes went past it and she stared at the ceiling in the room across the hall, Jeremy's eyes followed hers, noting the marble and gold-toned wallpaper. "So much detail."

"May I take your coats?" they heard a voice ask. Emma turned and started to unbutton her coat when she saw who it was. "Fred! What're you doing here?" she whispered.

"I told you at the theatre, I trust your instincts." He grinned. "And I thought this assignment might be a lot of fun."

She smiled slightly as she shrugged off her coat and handed it to him. Jeremy winked at Fred and handed him his coat. Claire and Thomas entered and handed over their coats, too.

Emma wandered through the grand hall and into the dining room. It was covered in custom wallpaper from the ceiling to the floor. There was a grand table and a fireplace that stood taller than Jeremy at the far end.

"You might go upstairs," Fred suggested. "There're more guests up there." They followed his direction and headed up, running their hands on the marble banister. Once they were upstairs, more stonework framed the walls and additional staircases.

"The house has seventeen types of marble, giving it the nickname of the 'Marble Palace'," Claire told Emma and Jeremy. "There's onyx, alabaster, carved and inlaid wood, glazed and patterned tiles."

"Wow," Jeremy said. "Ellis would love this."

"I think Papa worked on the house. They were one of the first truly fireproofed residences in the city." Fireproofing residences was something Ellis had worked hard for after the fire of 1871.

The party had spilled to other floors. Food and drink were spread out and the banisters and other surfaces were covered with Christmas greenery. There were Christmas trees in every room.

"Where to?" Jeremy asked.

"Just a sec." Emma went back downstairs and over to Fred. "Have you seen Lord Brunsby?"

His smile disappeared and he said, "No, I haven't. He might have already been here before I arrived."

"If you see him, will you let us know?" she asked.

"I'm sure we'll find him," he said before another couple coming in took his attention.

She went back to their group and they continued to stroll through the space. "There must be hundreds of people here," Jeremy lamented.

"You can wait for them to move to the private room," Claire told him.

"When?"

"Closer to midnight."

The quartet mingled and, at about ten o'clock, there was a large stir at the door. They walked to a staircase to watch. A group of men came in and their coats and top hats were taken.

"Where's Fred?" Emma asked, looking for the policeman.

"He might be on a break or helping out elsewhere," said Jeremy.

"I did notice the men moving around into different roles," she acknowledged, still looking for Fred.

"That's Brunsby." Claire nodded to a tall, dark-haired man.

Another man followed him in and Emma asked, "Is that Cole with them?"

"Looks like," Jeremy said.

"What's he doing?"

"He wanted to make sure Brunsby wasn't taken on the way here. The song doesn't say anything about a party."

An elegant woman joined Cole and, when she turned to remove her coat, Emma startled. "It's Amy!"

"Wow." Jeremy whistled.

"I didn't expect that," she said.

"Now that Brunsby's here, I'd assume whatever's going to happen will happen soon," Jeremy observed.

The group moved into the dining room for champagne and food. Cole and Amy stayed with them. Claire and Thomas broke away to circulate and discuss the foundation.

"We'll stay back and wait," Emma said.

"Ugh, these parties are so boring," Jeremy said, pulling on his tie. "Now I remember why we don't come to these things. 'Mister Tilden, so nice of you to attend our little soiree,'" he said in a faux upper-class accent. "'Ever so glad to be here, Mister Hogswallop. I believe you've met my fiancée, Penelope Candace?' 'Quite, quite. We should go hunting on the morrow, eh, what? A-ha. A-ha!'" He grimaced. "Yeesh," he continued in his normal voice, "gives me the jitters."

Emma rolled her eyes and straightened his tie. "Suck it up, buttercup. It's just this one night." She swatted his hand when he started to pull on his tie again. "Now, leave it alone. We'll be home soon enough."

"We're missing Christmas Eve with the family," he complained.

"I know, but if we save someone, they'll be able to see their family. And we have tomorrow. Did it arrive?" she asked anxiously.

"It did. It's in pieces and I'll be up late tonight getting it put together."

"You know, you could've asked Papa for help."

"I know, but I wanted to do this for Hen myself."

"You will."

He watched the clock and, as it moved forward, people got more inebriated. Fred appeared by his elbow. "Cole wanted me to tell you they're moving upstairs to the study."

Higher ground, thought Emma. "We're on our way."

Claire and Thomas started to follow, but Emma stopped them. "We need you to get Kelly and let him know what's happening." She nodded and took Thomas' arm. Emma and Jeremy headed up the stairs. Fred had disappeared again.

They arrived at the room and entered quietly. As the doors closed behind them, Emma turned and saw Fred behind her. He smiled. She turned back to the group. The men were talking and laughing. Cole stood to the side, watching the group. "Quiet so far," murmured Emma.

"Not for long," Fred commented. She frowned at him and started to ask, "What…"

"Father," Fred called to Lord Brunsby. Emma and Jeremy stared at him; he had an English accent.

"Fred?" she said and then it hit her. "Jeremy, it's Fred. Fred's the killer and the mole!" She started to move toward the man.

"I did not see that coming," Jeremy said, dumbfounded. He grabbed Emma and pulled her back to him.

"What are you doing?" she demanded. "Fred's the killer!"

Jeremy motioned to Fred's hands; he was carrying two very lethal-looking handguns.

"Father," Fred called again.

"Why, that sounds like Frederick," Brunsby said. He turned

NOTEBOOK MYSTERIES ~ THE TWELVE DAYS OF MURDER

toward him and, with a frown, he asked, "Freddy, what is the meaning of this?"

"This," Fred said, waving the guns at his father.

"Oh, put those away. You're liable to hurt yourself. Besides, can't you see we're busy?"

Fred laughed loudly. "Oh, you're always too busy for me aren't you, *Father*?"

Cole started to move towards Fred. He saw him and turned one of the guns to aim it at him. "Ah, Ah. Please, stay where you are. I included you, Emma, and Jeremy in this last part. You almost ruined my plans. The twelve days of murder. It was going to be glorious, but I only got five. But I'll get this one. Lord's a-leaping."

"What're you blabbering about?" Brunsby asked.

"You know the song, Father. The Twelve Days of Christmas."

"Doesn't that start tomorrow?" Brunsby asked, confused.

"Arghh. If I hear that one more time… Fine, yes, I was twelve days early. I wish everyone would just let it go!"

"So, what does the song have to do with me?"

"Well, it's the last day, of course, and I thought you could be there for your son to help me finish the song out properly."

"I don't understand, what's the twelfth day?"

A few voices rang out. "Twelve lords a-leaping."

Brunsby looked at his son. "How can I help?"

"By leaping, of course. I think you'll go first."

"Leaping? What do you mean? Leap out of the window?"

"Yes. Leap out the window. You disregarded my life, so now I disregard yours. You sent me over here and banished me from my family. You left me with no money and no place to live."

"You found your way; you became something on your own."

"I had to because the heir apparent, my *brother*, was going to get all of the money and the inheritance. What about me? Did you even care about me?"

"How can you do this to me?"

"Would you rather your friends go before you?" Fred sneered. His father's friends edged to the back of the room and away from the drama happening before them.

"Go to the window and open it, Father," Fred directed.

"But, Frederick. Son…"

Fred barked a laugh. "Now, you call me son. I begged you to let me stay in England."

"You needed to learn to make your own way. I thought it would be good for you."

"No, it was good for you. Now, out the window," Fred ordered.

Brunsby walked to the window and stood there.

"Now!" Cole shouted.

Emma pulled out her knife and threw it at Fred's arm. When it penetrated, he dropped the guns and went to his knees. Emma and Jeremy secured the guns. Cole went to the doors and let the Pinkerton men into the room. The men moved to get Brunsby and the other men out of the room.

"No, I want my father to stay here," whined Fred.

"Once again, my boy, you'll not get what you want," Brunsby said and turned to walk out with the Pinkerton men. After a few steps, he turned back. "You might think this is a little too late, but I was proud of you. Proud that you managed to make something of yourself over here. But now…" Brunsby turned his back on his son and walked away.

Fred lay on the floor, not moving, as Emma went over and knelt next to him. He was staring straight up, tears streaming down his face "Freddy," she said softly.

He turned his head to her. "It would've worked, you know, if you hadn't got involved. Everything was going according to plan."

"Is that why you joined the team?"

"After you got involved, I had to be on the squad," he said.

"You know this is the end."

"I know." He reached over and pulled out the knife. All the guns in the room were pointed at him. "Would you like your knife back?" he asked, wiping it on his jacket.

"Please," she said and took it from him. She reached over, put her hand into his jacket, and pulled out a bag of jewels. *So, Harvey was right.*

"I guess I can't keep those?"

"No, I don't think so."

"Eh, I didn't think so. You know, the guys who worked with me thought that was what this was about."

"What was it really about?"

"I'm not sure. Pride? I lost all sense of myself after I started." When she didn't say anything further, he asked, "Would you come to see me sometime?"

"Maybe," she said, standing. Jeremy pulled him to his feet.

"Just a second," she said and bent down to rip up her petticoat. She tied it quickly around his arm and they took him away.

"Why did you do that?" Jeremy asked.

"I figured I had one more good petticoat left, so I might as well use it."

Emma and Jeremy accompanied Fred to the station. Davies and Bill walked over to the wagon to take custody of Fred. They were silent as they walked him up the stoop.

"So glad we could help," called Emma.

"Eh, ignore them. It is Christmas Eve, and we need to get home." As they were walking down the street, the two clerks who owned the stores where they bought their gifts yelled to them from down the sidewalk.

Emma and Jeremy walked over to them. "What're you doing here on Christmas Eve?"

"We wanted to drop off some cakes and things for the officers."

"That's nice."

"Well, they got the animals out of our warehouse, and the area's been safer since then."

"That was your warehouse?" Emma asked. "Just who was that boy who warned you to close early?"

"It was..." the jewelry store clerk started, and he waved toward the station door. "It was him! Fred! He worked for us and managed our inventory in those warehouses."

CHAPTER 16

*C*hristmas day, early morning

"Is it together?" Emma whispered in the dark room.

"I believe so." Jeremy reached up and put a large bow on it.

"Bedtime," she said.

"A few hours, at least," he said with a wide yawn.

Hours later, there was a banging on Emma's door. "Father Christmas has come!"

"Stay up here, Hen," Emma called. "Don't go down yet!"

"I'll wait here for you."

"Go," she whispered to Jeremy.

He kissed her quickly. "See you on the other side," he said and moved to his room. Emma got up, closed the bookcase door, and opened the door to let Hen in. Hen ran in and jumped on the bed. "Merry Christmas, Hen."

"Merry Christmas, Emma."

Emma got dressed quickly and brushed her hair. "Ready to get Jeremy?"

"Yes!"

They went into the hallway and found Jeremy waiting. "Someone looking for me?"

They descended and heard many voices as they got closer to the sitting room. Amy and Cole walked into the foyer from the dining room. "Amy, I didn't think you were working today," Emma remarked.

"Oh, I'm not." Amy smiled, taking Cole's hand.

"She's with me," Cole said.

"That's wonderful. Merry Christmas to you both," Emma said and hugged them.

Amy looked nervously at Jeremy. He took her hands and said, "We're happy you're here with us this morning." She smiled and leaned onto Cole's shoulder.

Dora stepped out of the sitting room. "We have kids who want to open gifts. Get in here," she ordered.

They all walked in, and Hen stopped. "Whose is that?" she asked, pointing. It was a bike just like Emma's.

"I don't know, go check the tag," Jeremy told her.

The room stilled and watched as she approached it. "It has my name! Henrietta Evans Tilden!"

"Then it must be yours," Jeremy and Emma said.

"Merry Christmas, Hen!" called everyone from around the room.

Notebook Mysteries

Haunted Christmas

KIMBERLY
MULLINS

HISTORICAL NOTES

Frances O'Neill, the officer in this story was an interesting man. He was a cabin boy on an English merchant vessel at the age of 16. He immigrated to Illinois and in 1873 became a Chicago policeman. He was successful in his career and had the distinction of working for two different mayors as Chief of Police from 1901 to 1905.

Music was a large part of his identity, he was a flautist, fiddler and a piper in the Irish Community. O'Neill retired from the police force in 1905. After that, he devoted much of his energy to publishing the music he had collected. His musical works include:

- *O'Neill's Music of Ireland* (1903), containing 1,850 pieces of music
- *The Dance Music of Ireland* (1907), sometimes called, "O'Neill's 1001," because of the number of tunes included
- *400 tunes arranged for piano and violin* (1915)
- *Waifs and Strays of Gaelic Melody* (1922), 365 pieces
- *Irish Folk Music: A Fascinating Hobby* (1910). Appendix A contains *O'Farrells Treatise and Instructions on the Irish Pipes*,

published 1797-1800; appendix B is *Hints to Amateur Pipers* by Patrick J. Touhy.

• *Irish Minstrels and Musicians* (1913), biographies of musicians, including those from whom he collected tunes in Chicago.

He in fact did recruit many traditional Irish musicians into the police force. One of these was John Ennis.

John Ennis was active musically in Chicago from the 1890s to about 1919, and in New York City in the 1920s. He was a piper as well as a writer of poetry, verse, song lyrics, and articles. His youngest son, the baby was Tom Ennis, became a professional and well-known piper.

The Nickerson House where the final Lords a-leaping took place is a mansion built in Chicago in the 1800s. The three - story building is 24.000 square feet and was the most extravagant private residence in Chicago at the time of its completion. The building cost 450,000 to build (equating to more than 13billion in today's money).

The mansion's Italianate exterior is limestone and Ohio sandstone. The interiors are decorated with a large amount of marble (17 types, giving it the nickname of the "Marble Palace"), onyx, alabaster, carved and inlaid wood.

Tour: <u>Discover the Nickerson Mansion: The Inspiration Behind Historic Preservation in Chicago</u>

ABOUT THE AUTHOR

Kimberly Mullins is the author of series of books titled "Notebook Mysteries". Her stories are based on historical events occurring in 1871-1890's Chicago. She holds a BS in Biology and a MBA in Business. She lives in Texas with her husband and son. When she is not writing she is working as a Process Safety Engineer at a large chemical company. You can connect with her on her website www.kimberlymullinsauthor.com.

Photo Credit: Blessings of Faith Photography

X x.com/kremullins_kim

♪ tiktok.com/@krmullins14

www.ingramcontent.com/pod-product-compliance
Ingram Content Group UK Ltd.
Pitfield, Milton Keynes, MK11 3LW, UK
UKHW032334131224
452011UK00005B/74